"Collin, they know all the information I've gathered and everyone I've spoken with," Rebecca whispered.

Collin's gut clenched as a text confirmed what he'd suspected. Rebecca's car had been inventoried as part of gathering evidence at the crime scene, but her laptop was not there. Was this the work of a dirty cop?

"Your computer was never taken for evidence. It's gone." He took Rebecca's arm. "We should go. You can recount whatever you remember to the FBI and they can pick up the trail you started."

The sooner they got Rebecca's witness out of town and to the FBI, the better off they were going to be. If anything happened to her, or all three of them, the trafficking ring would have succeeded in tying up their loose ends and could continue on unscathed.

Collin opened the passenger door for Rebecca. But from the corner of his eye, he spotted a car approaching them, slowing down. The window lowered and the barrel of a gun protruded.

His instincts kicked in and he grabbed Rebecca and threw her to the ground behind the car as gunshots rang out, spraying his car with bullets...

Virginia Vaughan is a born-and-raised Mississippi girl. She is blessed to come from a large Southern family, and her fondest memories include listening to stories recounted around the dinner table. She was a lover of books from a young age, devouring tales of romance, danger and love. She soon started writing them herself. You can connect with Virginia through her website, virginiavaughanonline.com, or through the publisher.

Books by Virginia Vaughan

Love Inspired Suspense

Covert Operatives

Cold Case Cover-Up
Deadly Christmas Duty
Risky Return

Rangers Under Fire

Yuletide Abduction
Reunion Mission
Ranch Refuge
Mistletoe Reunion Threat
Mission Undercover
Mission: Memory Recall

No Safe Haven

RISKY RETURN

VIRGINIA VAUGHAN

HARLEQUIN® LOVE INSPIRED® SUSPENSE

Recycling programs
for this product may
not exist in your area.

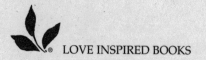

LOVE INSPIRED BOOKS

ISBN-13: 978-1-335-67909-3

Risky Return

www.Harlequin.com

Printed in U.S.A.

Thou in thy mercy has led forth the people
which thou hast redeemed: thou hast guided them
in thy strength unto thy holy habitation.
—*Exodus* 15:13

This book is dedicated to the men and women
who serve others unselfishly in all capacities and fields.
Thank you for what you do.

ONE

It was her.

Collin Walsh spotted Rebecca across the cashier stands at the local grocery store. He would know her anywhere, her long dark hair cascading over her shoulders as she picked up her groceries and walked out. He paid for his items then followed, watching her as she moved through the parking lot, oblivious to his presence. He'd wanted to play it cool when he saw her again but he wasn't sure he could. Should he approach her? Say hello? Or turn and walk away and not open those old wounds? He didn't even know what name she used these days. Had she kept the last name Walsh or gone back to her maiden name of Rebecca Mason?

She stopped at a blue Toyota Camry and dug through her purse, presumably for keys. He'd known he might see her when he'd returned to their hometown, but he hadn't expected the way his heart would be racing or how his mouth would be going dry when he finally did.

He looked away. If he was smart, he would walk back to his car and drive away, pretending he'd never seen her. But when he glanced at her again, he couldn't. She was beautiful. Just as beautiful as she'd been twelve years ago, and his brain reactivated memories he'd spent years pushing away. The feel of her in his arms. The taste of her lips. Running his hands through her hair. The way her eyes had gleamed as he'd slipped a pawnshop wedding ring on her long, slim finger.

Man, how he'd loved her.

Irritation bit at him. He'd faced down terrorists and some of the evilest people in the world in his jobs as both an army ranger and then a covert security specialist for the CIA, but saying a simple hello to the woman he'd once loved and married paralyzed him with fear.

His good sense kicked in and he walked in the opposite direction, toward his car. He'd already let her down once. No need to revisit his failure. Yet, he couldn't resist one last look. He turned back just in time to see a man approach her from behind, grab her and slam her head against the car.

Collin didn't even think as he dropped his bags and ran toward her, her cries of pain echoing in his ears. She slid to the ground but the man grabbed her hair and pulled her to her feet, this time whispering something in her ear. Collin couldn't hear what he'd said but it didn't matter. All that mattered was getting to Rebecca before this man could do any more damage.

He screamed at the attacker, who spun to face him then whipped out a knife and slung Rebecca to the ground before lunging at Collin. Oh, how he wished he had his gun with him, but he didn't need it to take down this man. It wasn't the first time he'd had to fight hand-to-hand with an armed assailant. His instincts kicked in, and he batted away the knife, knocking it from the attacker's hand as he kicked his legs out from under him. The attacker scrambled to his feet and took off running, disappearing around the corner of the store.

Collin didn't try to follow him. He was more concerned with making sure Rebecca was all right. He bent down beside her and called her name. When she didn't move, he carefully turned her over. Blood was running from a wound above her eye and her hands and arms were scraped from the pavement, but she was alive. Her eyes fluttered as she regained consciousness and his heart hammered against his chest when he saw her beautiful brown eyes staring back at him. She blinked several times then tried to sit up, grabbing her head in pain as she did.

"Take it easy," he said as he helped her.

"What—what happened?"

"A man attacked you as you were leaving the store. Don't you remember?"

She glanced at him again, but her eyes held more confusion than fear. He suspected his presence was probably only adding to it. "We should get you to a hospital."

"No!" The confusion seemed to clear from her face. "I don't need a hospital," she told him. "I need to go."

"You're bleeding."

She reached up and touched the gash then looked at the blood on her fingers. "I'm sure it's nothing."

He pulled out his phone. "I'm calling the police."

"Don't." She struggled to stand and he reluctantly helped her when it was obvious she wasn't going to remain still.

"I have to call. Someone intentionally tried to hurt you, Rebecca. You at least need someone to look at that gash and I know he slammed your head against the car. You should be examined by a doctor. You probably have a concussion. The police need to be notified and the man who did this needs to be found and held accountable."

"I just want to go home."

He thought she must still be in shock and didn't realize how close she'd come to being killed. Maybe she hadn't seen the knife her attacker wielded, but he was certain she'd felt her head slamming against the car. She reached for her car door handle, but Collin intervened, keeping it closed.

"You can't leave the scene of a crime and you certainly don't need to be driving in your condition." He should probably call someone on her behalf. Her family. A husband, perhaps. She would have had their sham of a marriage dissolved a long time ago and moved on with her life. They'd only been kids when she'd gotten pregnant and they'd run away together. She'd been barely eighteen and he'd been nineteen, not even old enough to get married in Mississippi without a parent's signature, so they'd crossed state lines and married in Louisiana, where eighteen was the legal age.

He'd left town after everything fell apart and hadn't looked back, so he'd never received any divorce papers, but he knew after certain public notices that she could have gotten one without his signature. He didn't see a ring on her hand and although he knew it didn't necessarily mean anything, he felt vindicated to know she was still single.

He should call her parents now, but he shuddered at the thought of even speaking to them. Collin would let the police handle that, or Rebecca, when she was able.

She looked up at him, the confusion returning to her face. "What are you doing here, Collin?"

It had to be a shock for her to see him again after all these years, but this didn't seem like the time to go into a lengthy description of why he'd returned. She was hurt and bleeding and had just been through a trauma.

He glanced at her belongings, now scattered on the ground. Her purse was still there and so were her keys. The attacker hadn't tried to rob her or even steal her car. This attack had been personal. "Who did this, Rebecca? And why would anyone want to hurt you?"

Rebecca's head was still swimming when the paramedics and police arrived. She hadn't wanted them there, but she'd agreed because she didn't want to tell him about Missy. She allowed herself to be helped into the ambulance and her gash and scrapes tended to. Her head was pounding and she was having trouble focusing on what was happening. But she had to keep her wits about her. A girl's life depended on it.

An unmarked cruiser pulled up to the scene and Kent Morris got out, his hair and clothes neat and orderly. He'd always dressed impeccably ever since high school and she knew he was ambitious and had recently been made an investigator with the sheriff's office. He approached Collin first and started asking questions.

Collin Walsh! A new rush of confusion washed over her. What was he even doing here? She hadn't seen him in twelve years, but today he'd appeared out of nowhere and swooped in to save her life. There was no denying it was him. He was older, but he had the same strong features and beautiful green eyes. He was a shadow from her past. Her first love. Her high school boyfriend, then later her husband when they'd eloped after discovering she was pregnant. And the father of the baby lost to them both before he was even born.

She'd often imagined that if their baby had

lived, if she hadn't miscarried him, he would he have had Collin's smile and curly hair. He would have been twelve now, nearly a teen-ager and as witty and charming as Collin had been at that age. She tamped down that train of thought. She couldn't go there. She wouldn't, because it hurt too much to even imagine.

The paramedic finished bandaging her up. "You should go to the hospital to get checked out."

"I'm fine," Rebecca assured her. "I don't need to go."

"If you lost consciousness, you might have a concussion."

"I said I'm fine." She didn't relish the idea of sitting in a hospital for hours on end. Her head hurt but it was nothing a few Tylenol couldn't help. She had to get back to Missy Donovan. Rebecca had promised her food and a safe place to stay until they figured out what to do and whom they could trust with her story. She'd picked up something for her at a drive-through when she took the teen to the motel, but she'd hoped to return with more food and supplies tonight. Those groceries were now scattered around the parking lot.

Kent approached her, followed closely by Collin. His green eyes studied her, and she was suddenly self-conscious. He certainly wasn't seeing her at her best. Her face felt swollen and the bandage on her forehead couldn't be attractive.

Stop it. It didn't matter what she looked like to Collin. Not anymore. Not since he'd abandoned her after she'd lost the baby.

Kent spoke first. "Hey, Rebecca, Collin filled me in on what happened here. Did you see the man who attacked you?"

"I didn't see anything." It wasn't a lie. The man had blindsided her. She'd never seen his face, but that didn't mean she didn't have an idea who'd attacked her.

"Well, I've asked Collin to work with a sketch artist to see if we can identify this man. We're also pulling prints off your car and pulling security footage from the store. Don't you worry, we'll find this guy."

"I appreciate that, Kent."

"Any idea why someone would want to hurt you, Rebecca?"

Now was the time to come clean about the notes, the threats, even the girl she was helping hide out in the Batesville Motel, but something stopped her. Missy had told her that the police were involved in the trafficking ring she'd escaped from two nights ago.

And her attacker's eerie warning to mind her own business entered her thoughts.

Collin noticed her hesitation. He could always see right through her. "What is it, Rebecca? Are you in some kind of trouble?"

All she wanted was to go home and crawl into bed and forget this day had ever happened, but she knew she couldn't. "I've been receiving some threats lately. Letters and messages."

"What did they say?"

"They warned me to stop what I was doing or I would be sorry."

"And what is it they think you're doing, Rebecca?" Collin asked.

She saw the doubt in his face—he was wondering if she'd gotten involved in something illegal. Could he really believe she would have changed that much? Had he? "It's complicated."

"Uncomplicate it," Kent insisted.

She looked at them both. The last few days had been a haze of suspicion and doubt. She didn't know who she could trust in this town anymore. Even her own father was a suspect after Missy had told her about seeing the name Mason Industries, her father's company, on the building where she'd been held.

"Four months ago, a pregnant teen in my

care went missing. Kent, you classified her as a runaway, but I never stopped looking for her. I think whoever has her wants me to stop looking."

"You believe she was abducted?" Collin asked. "Do you have any idea who took her?"

She didn't see an ounce of doubt in Collin's expression and she liked that, but she had to remember she hadn't seen this man in twelve years, not since the day he'd walked out of their marriage and left her abandoned and alone in New Orleans. "When can I go home?" Rebecca asked, ignoring his question.

Kent gave her an annoyed look. "I still have some questions to ask you once we finish processing this scene and I need to see those threatening notes, Rebecca. You should have come to me when you received the first one."

"I know I should have, but you never believed me that Missy wasn't a runaway."

"I might have changed my mind after seeing those."

"I'm sorry, Kent. Please, I just want to go home. My head is killing me."

She feared he was about to give her the you-need-to-go-to-the-hospital spiel again, but he sighed instead. "I can have a deputy take you home."

"That won't be necessary," Collin said. "I'll take her home."

Rebecca wasn't sure how she felt about that. Collin had swooped back into her life all of a sudden and she hadn't even gotten her equilibrium back enough to process his return. Now, he was offering to drive her home?

He held out his hand and she took it, but as she stood, the world around her began to spin. Her knees buckled and she fell, but Collin was there in a shot, wrapping his strong arms around her and keeping her vertical. She soaked in the smell of his musky aftershave as she leaned into him.

"I'll help you," he said, his voice gentle and reassuring.

She allowed him to guide her to his car, but as she slid inside she realized she didn't have the food she'd come here for. She pressed her head against the back of the seat. She wasn't up for any more shopping today. Hopefully Missy would be okay until the morning.

Collin slid into the driver's seat, started the car and turned out of the parking lot. She still couldn't believe she was sitting beside Collin Walsh. It was too unreal to be anything but a dream. And how many times had she dreamed about this man reappearing in her life through the years? Now, he had.

She reached out and touched his arm just to reassure herself this was real. He covered her hand with his and the weight of it against hers convinced her it was. Collin Walsh was back in town and back in her life.

He squeezed her hand but the furrowing of his brow told her he was worried. "Are you sure you're okay?"

"I will be." She moved her hand and turned away. She couldn't sit here drooling over Collin. She had to get back to Missy. But his reappearance in her life was something she hadn't planned on. "I didn't know you were back in town," Rebecca said. In fact, she hadn't heard of him being back in their hometown in years.

"My mom passed away a few months ago. She'd been in a nursing home for years. I thought it was time to clean out her house and put it on the market."

His mother. Of course. Rebecca had visited with her often, keeping tabs on Collin and his jaunts around the world in the army, reading the letters he'd sent home to his mom until her health forced her to be moved. "I'm sorry about your mother. I always liked her."

He gave a slight smile and glanced at her. "Thank you. She always liked you, too."

If only her parents had been as easygoing

as his mother, things might have ended differently between them. They had never liked Collin, even going so far as to forbid Rebecca from seeing him. That hadn't stopped her. Nothing could have stopped her from marrying Collin Walsh back then…and nothing had.

And she'd paid a big price for doing so. She'd lost her husband, her baby and her happy future.

"I couldn't believe it when I saw you in the store," he said. "Honestly, I was trying to decide if I should say hi or not when I saw that man grab you."

So he'd considered not even speaking to her? It stung her to know she meant so little to him when she'd once loved him so much. But she was grateful he'd been there. She didn't know what her attacker would have done if Collin hadn't intervened. Would he have used that knife he'd flashed at her? Or had this attack only been a warning? She wrung her hands and looked out the window. Was he out there somewhere following them? She was suddenly very glad Collin had offered to take her home.

"Thank you for helping me." A thousand questions popped into her mind that she wanted to ask him. She'd thought about him often throughout the years, and wondered where he was and what he was doing. "Did I hear you joined the army?"

"I did. I even became an army ranger."

That was impressive.

"But I left the service three years ago. I've been working private security ever since."

"Like being a bodyguard?"

"Sort of, but on a global scale. I was overseas when Mom passed away. Fortunately, her sister was with her when she died."

How terrible that he hadn't been able to be there with his mother. However, she knew his mom had suffered from dementia and hadn't known anyone for several years. Still, she couldn't imagine not being home when her own mother had died of cancer five years earlier.

"What about you? What are you doing these days?"

"I work for the court system. I'm a psychologist specializing in child welfare. I act as a representative for children who come through the courts, usually those who've been removed from their homes and gone into the foster care system." It wasn't the career her parents had hoped for her, but she enjoyed her work and the kids she helped. Only now, helping one of them had placed her life in danger.

She glanced out the window again and still saw no one behind them, but would she even know how to recognize a tail if she had one?

Collin reached over and covered her hands with his right hand again. "No one is following us," he assured her. "I've been watching. Whoever it was that attacked you is gone."

She gave him a warm smile. He always could reassure her.

"I knew you would do good things," he told her. "You always had a good heart."

But not good enough to keep him around. She grimaced at that thought as their past and present collided. She had to keep her focus on today and what was happening now. "I enjoy my work. I've gotten quite close to some of the kids I work with."

"No kids of your own?"

She stared at him. How could he even ask that when they were still technically married? The day he'd left, her dreams of family and children were placed permanently on hold. "No, of course not."

She pointed out her driveway and Collin pulled into it and got out. She got out, too, her balance steadier but still off-kilter. He held on to her arm as he walked her toward the front door.

"Are you sure you're okay to be alone? You don't want to go to the hospital?"

"No. I'll be fine. It's only a cut. I'm more shaken up than anything." She pulled out her keys. There were so many things she wanted to say to him, to ask him, but none of them would come out. He'd come back to town not to see her, but to clean up his mother's house and finally sever his last connection to her and this town. She wouldn't intrude on his life. And she wouldn't drag him into her mess. She forced herself to move away from him.

"Thank you for your help, Collin. It was good to see you again." It didn't sound like enough after all they'd been through. They'd never even talked about their marriage or the baby they'd lost. It had all just seemed to fade away in the years they'd been apart.

She glanced up at him and thought she saw something more in his eyes, something he wanted to say. He stepped closer and her knees weakened, and it wasn't from the bash on her head. He still had that power over her. But he didn't say whatever was on his mind. Instead, he stepped back away from her. "It was good to see you, too, Rebecca." Such simple words and yet they stung her. It was really true. Everything they'd ever had was over. She turned, her hands shaking as she pushed the key into the door and stepped inside. She leaned against the door as she closed it, heaving a sigh as she closed the door on her life with Collin as well.

She opened her eyes and a scream escaped her lips.

He turned and ran back toward the house at the sound of Rebecca's scream. Pushing open the door, he saw her huddled in the corner. Written in paint on the opposite wall were the threatening words *Today was only the beginning*. Someone had been here, inside her home.

"Stay here," he warned her. "I'm going to check the house to make sure he's not still here."

Again, he wished for his gun, but he was ready if he saw anyone hiding. He checked room by room but saw no evidence that anyone was still here. He did find broken glass by her living room window. That must have been how the intruder got inside.

"No one is here," he said, returning to the front hall, where she was still crouched, her face pale and her eyes wide with fright.

Rebecca was small and frail in his arms

as he helped her to the couch and his instinct was to pull her to him for comfort. But he checked that feeling, since they weren't in a relationship any longer.

Tears rolled down her cheeks. "They were in my house."

"I know, but we'll find them." He took out his phone and called Kent, explaining the situation. He promised to come by as soon as he wrapped up the scene at the parking lot.

Collin hurried into the kitchen and returned with a glass of water for her. Her hands were shaking as she held it and took a sip.

He cringed as he thought about the man who had attacked her earlier. Had he been the one inside her home as well? Someone was after her and they knew where she lived. "You said you had threatening letters? Can I see them?"

She nodded then got up and walked on shaky legs into the kitchen. She opened a drawer and pulled out a plastic bag. Inside were several pieces of paper with letters cut out of magazines and glued onto them to form words of warnings. They were old-school and that was notable, but it was also harder to trace than emails or text messages. The notes were chillingly to-the-point.

Mind your own business.

Stay out of our way.

Stop investigating or you will die.

He shuddered at the threat. She'd stumbled across a serious and potentially dangerous person. And they'd already tried to make good on their threats. Fear crept up his neck—fear for her and her safety. "We should get these to Kent. When did they start coming?"

"I found the first one on my car windshield eight days ago. The next two were here at my house."

He didn't like the fact that whoever was after her knew where she lived and had been inside her house. "Do you live alone?"

"Yes."

"Any pets?"

"No. Why?"

"Dogs are the best alarm system you can have." He slid into the chair opposite her.

"Do you have a dog?"

It struck him as an oddly personal question that had nothing to do with keeping her safe. "No, I don't." He wasn't generally home enough to take on the commitment of a pet. That might be changing soon however, after his team's actions in Libya. They'd been working security for a covert CIA base when an attack on an American embassy occurred only a few miles away. Collin recalled seeing the smoke from intentionally set fires even from their base, but they'd been told to stand down, as the government had decided its CIA interests were more important than the Americans dying nearly in front of them. His team had defied those orders and gone in, anyway. Assuming the CIA continued to utilize Security Operations Abroad operatives, Collin doubted his contract, and those of the others on his team, would be extended.

It looked like he was back on American soil for good.

He heard a car pulling into her driveway and walked to the window. "It's Kent. How did that guy get to be a cop?"

"He's worked his way up the ranks. He says it's all he's ever wanted to be."

Kent entered the house, glanced at the threat painted on the wall and whistled. "You have angered someone, haven't you, Rebecca?"

Collin pointed to the window that had been shattered. "That's how he got inside. And the threatening letters she told you about are on the table. They're pretty intense."

He walked over and glanced at the letters

then took out his phone. "I'll have Forensics come by and process this scene."

"How long will that take?" Collin asked.

Kent shrugged. "A couple of hours. We'll try to pull prints off the windowsill and the wall."

"Good. I'll take Rebecca and go to the hardware store for something to board up the window and some paint to cover that."

"We should be done by the time you get back. I'll also have these letters sent to the lab for examination. Maybe we can pull some prints off them."

Collin glanced at Rebecca. Even though she'd stopped shaking, she still looked so fragile sitting in that chair. He wanted to get her out of here, fix everything and make it like it was before to make her feel better, but he knew paint and boards couldn't fix this.

She was in danger and he couldn't make that go away with only a trip to the hardware store.

Collin did his best to keep Rebecca's mind off what was going on at her house and, for the most part, he succeeded. Except she knew very well what the lumber and paint were for.

Rebecca stole a moment at the hardware store to slip into the bathroom and phone

Missy to let her know she'd been held up and wouldn't be returning to the motel tonight. She didn't tell Missy about the attack in the parking lot or the threatening message on her wall. The girl didn't need the added worry and Rebecca wasn't entirely sure she could make it through that conversation without breaking down herself. She touched the tender spot on her forehead where her attacker had slammed her head against the car and knew Missy would find out about it tomorrow, anyway. She certainly couldn't hide the bruises from her.

"I'm fine," Missy assured her. "I'm going to try to sleep."

"Good. Be sure to keep the door locked and don't answer it for anyone. I'll see you tomorrow." Rebecca ended the call then rejoined Collin at the cash register.

A text message from Kent alerted them that it was safe to return to the house. When Rebecca reentered her home, she flinched at the threatening message still there, but then she saw fingerprint dust everywhere. Kent's people had left a mess but at least they were gone.

Collin got to work boarding up the window that had been broken. "Tomorrow, I'll have someone come out and replace the glass."

"Thank you," Rebecca said, grateful to

have someone else handling these things. She was still shaking inside from knowing someone had not only attacked her, but had also been inside her house. It felt different now, like a sacred trust had been broken. Having Collin with her eased that feeling, but how comfortable would she feel once he was gone?

He opened the can of paint he'd purchased and began covering up the threatening words, but after one coat, it still seeped through. Evil always did.

He shook his head. "Guess it's going to take another coat. I'll let this one dry then start on another."

She heated up the takeout containers of ribs they'd picked up and they sat down to eat. It was surreal sitting across from Collin eating a meal. He was so different yet so much the same. He didn't have to be here with her, yet he'd chosen to stay and help without being asked. She wasn't surprised he'd made a good soldier; he'd always had a heart to help others.

She had to stop thinking so fondly of him. This was the man who'd promised to love her for all time then abandoned her with no word after she lost the baby. No amount of boarding up windows or painting a wall could change that. He'd left her and no matter how nice he was being today, she couldn't let herself trust him or she'd be devastated again when he left.

They ate in silence; the awkwardness between them filled the air. Despite the pain of their past relationship, he'd shown up today and she'd once known everything about him. She knew very little about him now except the basics he'd shared—he'd been an army ranger, now worked private security and was back in town to deal with his late mother's estate.

"So tell me something about you," she said.

He shrugged. "There's not much to tell. My work keeps me traveling. Or at least, it used to."

"You're not working overseas anymore?"

He shrugged. "That's something that is still up in the air. What about you, Rebecca? How is your life?"

"It's good. I'm happy."

"You never remarried?"

She looked at him, confused. "How could I when I'm still married to you?"

He choked on his food then dropped it, looking dismayed as he stared at her. "What do you mean? You never got a divorce?"

She was surprised by his shock. Of course, he'd assumed she had taken care of it. She should have, instead of letting this joke of a marriage continue, yet she'd never been able to bring herself to file the papers. "At first, I was too heartbroken to even think about it. Then I was just too ashamed. I never told anyone that we got married. My father would have been so angry and at the time, I just couldn't deal with it. My family still doesn't know. After a while, it seemed easier to keep it a secret. I never told them about the baby, either."

He leaned back in his seat and sighed. "No one knows?"

She shook her head. It seemed wrong to never mention their child and she often felt guilty for keeping it a secret, but whenever she tried to think about it or mention it to someone, it brought back all the pain and heartache of that day. "Sometimes it feels like it never happened, but I know it did."

She stood and cleared away the containers, hoping activity would ease the tension between them. She picked up a towel and started wiping down the counters, vaguely aware of him standing behind her.

"Rebecca, I—I'm sorry."

"Don't." She turned around to face him. "This day has been too much for me, Collin. I can't deal with you, too. I just want to go to bed and forget this day ever happened."

He backed away from her, digging his hands into his pockets in a way she remembered he did whenever he'd been rebuked. "I'll finish up that second coat then I'll be out of your way."

She gave a sigh of relief and thanked him when the second coat of paint covered the ugly marks. Collin cleaned up then made certain the house was secure before he left. The place felt empty with him gone, but she knew it was for the best. It felt good to finally tell someone else what she'd been struggling with. It was like a burden lifted from her shoulders. She wasn't alone in this. But despite how grateful she was that he'd been here today, she couldn't risk her heart by having him around long-term. It stunned her that she still had such strong feelings for him even after all this time. It had to be because of the stress of the day's events.

She got ready for bed then slipped between the blankets, her body screaming for rest but her mind still wide-awake and the pounding in her head unimaginable. How would she ever sleep with all that had happened to her today? And she still had to decide what to do with Missy. The girl had shown up on her doorstep two nights ago, frightened and claiming she'd been abducted by people who'd wanted her baby. The timing was right. Missy had been six months pregnant when she'd vanished, she'd been missing for months, and she was certainly now not pregnant. But who were these people after her and how was Rebecca going to protect her if she wouldn't go to the police?

Her mind turned back to Collin despite the fact that she was trying not to think about him. Seeing him again today evoked so many emotions she'd spent years trying to manage. Grief for the loss of her child. Heartbreak over the way he'd abandoned her. She should hate him. Why, then, was falling into his arms all she wanted to do?

She finally drifted off but her sleep was fitful and restless, her dreams wrought with all the pain and fear that had rocked her day. She jerked awake but was certain it hadn't been the dream that woke her.

Panic filled her as she realized a figure was standing over her bed.

Rebecca scrambled up but the man's hands grabbed her and wrapped around her neck. He pinned her down, choking her. She gasped for breath, fear rising in her. She kicked and clawed at him, struggling to get free, and felt her nails digging into flesh through the dark mask he wore.

God, help me.

She couldn't go out like this. She couldn't leave Missy to fight these people alone. She wasn't going to let them win! One of her kicks landed, sending the man rolling off her. She reached for her bedside lamp and crashed it over his head. He hit the floor, groaning in pain as Rebecca ran. She hurried through the house to the front door and ran outside, not stopping to look back to see if her attacker was following. She crossed the lawn to her next-door neighbor's house and knocked until he answered. He was groggy after being pulled from sleep.

"Rebecca, what's wrong?"

Only then did she allow herself to fall apart. "He attacked me!"

TWO

The call from Kent had Collin dressed and heading toward Rebecca's house in mere moments. He saw her when he pulled up and parked. She was sitting in the ambulance as a forensics team cleaned beneath her nails. As he neared her, the ugly bruises around her neck were just starting to form, to go along with the ones on her face. She looked pale and weak, but he knew she wasn't. She'd survived this attack by fighting back and that took courage and strength. She'd always been strong—the strongest woman he'd ever known. She'd defied her father to be with him and that had taken real courage.

She glanced up and saw him and tears sprang to her eyes. His own rush of emotion nearly toppled him and an anger flashed through him that he hadn't felt in a long, long time. Then the guilt washed over him. He should have stayed, offered to sleep on the couch, and if she'd refused his offer, he should have slept in his car outside. He would have been there to protect her, to see when some nutjob broke in and tried to harm her.

Kent approached him and Collin shook his hand. "Thanks for calling me."

"I figured you would want to know. She's okay, not seriously hurt. She put up a good fight, even got us some possible DNA by scratching his face."

"Do you know who did this?"

"No, he wore a mask and was gone when the first car responded. We're canvassing the neighborhood to see if anyone saw anything suspicious and Forensics is back inside processing the house. We'll find something."

He spotted them closing the ambulance doors and after a moment the vehicle drove away with her inside. Collin walked into the house and followed Kent into the bedroom, where a team was already working. There was clear evidence of a struggle—the lamp broken on the floor and blood on the carpet, blankets in disarray. She'd fought for her life in this room. Three attacks in less than twelve hours. He shuddered at the thought.

He'd seen evil before, more times than he could count, but this was personal. This was his Rebecca who had been attacked. He turned and walked from the scene, his stomach roiling with anger and guilt.

Kent followed him. "You okay, Collin?"

He wasn't, but he would be once he tracked down whoever was after her. "I'm going to the hospital to make certain Rebecca is okay."

He couldn't even allow himself to think about what could have happened here tonight. He'd failed her years ago when she'd needed him most. He'd promised to provide for her and for the baby, but he hadn't been able to. He'd struggled as a young man fresh out of high school to find work that would support a wife and a child. He still recalled the feeling of helplessness knowing that he couldn't even keep the lights on regularly. And when she'd lost the baby, he'd lost her. She'd closed up and he was certain she knew the mistake she'd made in marrying him.

He could never recover from those failures of his youth, but he couldn't just walk away knowing she was in danger. She was in trouble and he now had the skills to keep her safe.

He turned back to Kent. "Can you place a deputy at the hospital for her safety?"

"We're short-staffed," Kent told him. "I'll never get the sheriff to authorize around-the-clock protection, especially when he knows her father has the money to hire someone."

Her father. Collin hadn't considered that. He was surprised Bob Mason hadn't already hired someone to protect her if he knew she was in danger. But as he looked at Rebecca's house, he had to wonder what he knew. It was a modest home, a surprise to him. She'd grown up in opulence, living in one of the biggest homes in town. Her parents had always had money and she'd been denied very little in her life. He was one of only a few things they'd tried to deny her. He'd expected her to at least live in a fashionable condo or a higher-class neighborhood. Even the car he'd seen her getting into, a simple Toyota Camry, seemed modest. It was a far cry from the BMW convertible she'd gotten for her sixteenth birthday. Was it possible she was estranged from her dad? Had he cut her off? Because of him and the six months they'd spent together after running off to get married? No, from what he gathered from Rebecca today, if she and her father were no longer close, it was because she was the one who'd done it.

All he knew was that it couldn't be a coincidence he was in town at the same time Rebecca was in trouble. Collin hadn't always put much faith in God, but He had to be the reason for this reconnection with Rebecca.

Collin couldn't leave town until he knew she was safe.

He followed the ambulance to the ER and sat in the waiting room while the doctors examined her. A nurse approached him. "Sir, are you here with Rebecca Mason?"

He stood. "I am. How is she?"

"She has a mild concussion and some bruising but she's fortunate there were no greater injuries. You can go back to see her for a few minutes."

He followed the nurse to a room, then pushed open the door. Rebecca was sitting up in a hospital bed, but her skin was pale and dark circles had formed around her eyes. It pained him to see how small and frail she looked and his first instinct was to pull her into his arms and hold on to her. He shoved away that thought and slid a chair to her bedside.

"How are you feeling?" he asked her, unable to stop the impulse to reach for her hand.

She didn't pull it away. In fact, she clasped his, her long fingers cool to the touch. "I'm okay. Just shaken up."

"That's twice today someone has tried to hurt you, Rebecca. Three, if you count the threatening message. I'm sorry. I should have stayed with you."

"This is not your fault, Collin. You had no idea this would happen."

"I should have suspected something."

"You can't blame yourself for everything, Collin. Not everything in life is your fault."

He looked up at her and they both seemed to realize how easily they'd slipped into matters of the past. She knew him so well, but this time, he was certainly at fault for not protecting her.

Suddenly, he felt awkward being there with her. She needed rest and time to recover from the attacks. "I'll go now and let you get some sleep." He stood but she didn't release his hand. He glanced back at her.

Tears filled her eyes. "I'm glad you're here," she told him.

He was confused. Should he leave or stay? His heart urged him to remain by her side, but he wasn't sure that was for the best. She was injured and concussed, wasn't thinking properly, and he didn't want to take advantage of that. And she'd been clear earlier at the house that she didn't want him around.

Thankfully he didn't have to choose. The door to her room opened and a nurse walked in. "That's long enough. The patient needs her rest."

Their moment was broken and their time

together over. "I should go. I hope you feel better soon, Rebecca," he said as he headed for the door.

He shouldn't have remained so long and he never should have gone back there to see how she was. He should have gotten into his car and gone about his business once the ambulance had taken her away. Only, she was his business—at least she had been—and even though he knew they could never be together again, he didn't want to live in a world without Rebecca Mason in it.

Rebecca pushed back the blanket and got up, intending to get her clothes and get out of here. She wasn't safe and she had to let Missy know what was happening, but she had to be smart. She couldn't lead these people to Missy or they would both be in danger.

"What do you think you're doing?" the nurse asked.

"I'm leaving. I'll sign whatever papers I need to sign, but I have to go."

"You're not going anywhere."

She was about to yank out the IV when the nurse clamped her hand down on Rebecca's arm, her fingers digging into her skin. Rebecca looked up and saw nothing but contempt in the woman's face. "I said you're not going anywhere," the nurse insisted again. This time, her words had a bite to them— more bite than Rebecca would have expected from a nurse trying to stop a patient from leaving against medical orders. The woman stood like a brick wall between her and the door, and the determination in her face was evident. "Get back in that bed."

But she wasn't going to be pushed around. She had to get to Missy. "I'm leaving," she said again.

Only this time, the woman grabbed her arm and twisted it, causing Rebecca to cry out and fall to her knees. The nurse leaned over her and warned, "You're not going anywhere, Rebecca. You're never going anywhere again."

The hatred in her face frightened her and Rebecca knew something was very wrong. This couldn't just be about her leaving. The nurse grabbed her other arm and shoved her to the bed, then grabbed her feet and slung her into it, pinning her down with her body. Rebecca struggled to get free but the woman was too big and strong for her to get loose. The nurse pulled restraints from her pocket and managed to get Rebecca's hands clamped down, then moved to her feet. Rebecca frantically pulled at them, trying to get loose. She screamed for help and kicked and dodged, but this woman wasn't fazed. She must have done this a hundred times before.

"What are you doing?" Rebecca asked as the woman pulled a syringe from her pocket and injected it into Rebecca's IV. "What is that?"

She leaned over her and sneered. "Just a little something to shut you up. You should have listened to the warnings we sent you in those notes," she said. "Now, you'll go to sleep and never wake up. It'll look like you suffered a heart attack from your previous injuries."

Rebecca jerked, realizing what this was. Murder! Was this woman even a nurse here, or was she posing as one to kill her?

"Someone help me!" she cried, aiming her voice toward the doorway.

The nurse laughed. "No one is coming to save you, Rebecca. As far as the nurses are concerned, you're just another out-of-control patient that had to be restrained. By the time anyone checks on you, it'll be too late."

She turned on the television, adjusting the volume so that it was loud, then pulled the cord that ran from the nurse's call button to the bed out of the wall and dropped it to the floor out of reach. She turned and walked out, switching off the lights as she left.

When the door swung shut and the room

went dark, terror rushed through Rebecca. The first effects of the drug the nurse had injected into her began to appear. The room started spinning and her legs and arms lost their will to fight. But she couldn't give up. If she fell asleep, she was dead. She had to keep struggling until someone heard her.

She pulled at the restraints, forcing herself to keep going. Her life began to flash through her mind, specifically her life with Collin and the image of what could have been if only she'd been stronger and more committed. If only she hadn't lost the baby.

Nausea rolled through her. Her body wanted to give in to the drug, but her mind continued to fight. She didn't want to die. Her right hand at last slipped through one of the restraints and she was able to sit up a bit to loosen the other. But the call button on the floor was unplugged and useless. She loosened the restraints on her feet and forced her legs to move. They did, slipping over the side of the bed, but when she tried to stand, they wouldn't support her and she fell, hitting the floor with a thud. Pain shot through her. She cried out but even she knew her cries were weak and would never reach past the closed doorway.

She was going to die right here in this room and no one would know.

God, where are You? Why had He left her and allowed so many terrible things to happen to her?

And where was Collin when she needed him?

She couldn't even voice those questions as the darkness pulled her away.

Leaving Rebecca's side had been difficult, but the decision to remain at the hospital was a no-brainer. Collin planted himself in the waiting room. He had a direct view of her room and he wasn't leaving the hospital until he knew she was safe. His cell phone rang and he answered it and heard Kent's voice.

"Are you at the hospital? How is Rebecca?"

"Aside from a concussion, the nurse said she would be fine. I'm going to hang around for a while to make sure she's okay."

"She's definitely crossed some dangerous people and if today's attacks prove anything, it's that they mean business. I'll swing by there as soon as I'm finished at her house."

"I'll be here," Collin told him.

Deciding to check on Rebecca again, he pushed open the door to her room and poked his head inside but didn't see her. She was supposed to be resting, but the bed was empty. He was about to go find the nurse when he spotted something on the floor by the bed. He stepped back inside. It was a foot poking out from beneath the bed.

His heart dropped and he ran around the bed. Rebecca was on the floor unconscious. The nurse's call button was on the floor beside her, useless. He ran to the door and swung it open. "I need help in here!" he hollered toward the nurses' station then ran back to Rebecca.

He kneeled beside her and felt for a pulse, his heart hammering against his chest. This couldn't be happening. Not again.

A nurse hurried into the room and felt for a pulse, then reached over the bed and pressed an emergency button. Moments later, a team of people rushed in.

Collin was pushed aside as they lifted her to the bed and began working on her. Panic filled him. She looked so still and lifeless. He'd seen death, been around it, even caused it before, but seeing Rebecca this way staggered him.

"I need you to go wait in the family waiting area," the nurse who'd arrived first instructed him. "We'll find you when we know what's happening."

He didn't want to go, didn't want to leave her, but the nurse nudged him from the room and closed the door. He stood there a few moments then stumbled to the waiting area and fell into a chair. He put his head in his hands.

His instinct was to pray, but he didn't even remember how. All he could do was cry out in his heart to God not to allow death to take her. It wasn't fair that he'd bumped into Rebecca today, gotten to see her again, only to have her snatched away.

After what seemed like an eternity, the nurse appeared in the doorway. Two security guards followed her.

"How is she?" Collin asked.

"She's stable for now but I need you to remain here. These guards will stay with you. The police will be coming to question you soon."

"The police? Why?" He could see her hesitancy to tell him anything. "Please, what's happening?" He mentally kicked himself. Why had he left her tonight?

"Miss Mason regained consciousness long enough to tell us a woman was in her room and injected something into her IV. We're treating her and the police have been contacted. They're on their way."

Collin shuddered. Another attack? That made three in one day. She should have been safe here in the hospital, just as she should have been safe at her home, but someone was determined to keep her silent about whatever it was she knew about the missing girl.

Only minutes later, Kent arrived looking as tired and rattled as Collin felt. "What happened here?" he asked. "I was on my way when I got the call about a possible poisoning?"

"I don't know the details. All I know is I entered her room to see her and she was on the floor unconscious. The nurse said she'd been injected with something. Rebecca told her a woman was in her room."

"These people aren't messing around. I'm having those threatening notes sent to the lab for prints. Hopefully we can pull some off them."

The same nurse that had given him the brush-off approached Kent and relayed what had happened. "She was apparently injected with some kind of drug but it's not charted and no one is admitting to going into her room or giving her anything. In fact, the doctor had ordered a CT scan and we were waiting for them to come take her. She shouldn't have been receiving any medication until that was complete. We gave her a drug that counteracts most narcotics and she's stable now." She glanced at Collin. "If you hadn't found her when you did, she probably would have died."

Earlier, this nurse had treated him like a suspect. He felt vindicated but couldn't dwell on that. She didn't know him and had been right to be suspicious of everyone, yet saving Rebecca's life seemed to have garnered him less suspicion by this nurse. Plus, Rebecca had said a woman attacked her. Collin turned to Kent. "Three attempts on her life in one day. Are you sure your boss can't authorize a guard by her door?"

Kent rubbed his face. "I'll check into it."

The nurse continued. "In the meantime, hospital security will be placed at her door. No one will go in or out of that room without permission from me and that includes any service personnel or housekeeping."

"Thank you," Collin stated, grateful for her diligence. "May I see her now?"

She nodded. "Sure. She's out of danger but she's sleeping. I'd say she's just plain worn out from the day's events."

As Collin headed for Rebecca's hospital room, he heard Kent tell the nurse he wanted to see all her records and wanted a list of all people who'd been in and out of her room. Good. He hoped Kent's investigation would lead to something concrete, something that would identify the person or people trying to hurt Rebecca.

He stepped inside her room and his heart broke as he saw her lying so frail on the bed. He shuddered, remembering those letters and the way he'd found her sprawled on the floor. But at least she was breathing okay now. He slid into a chair and watched her, listening to her steady breathing. He wasn't leaving her side again, at least not until he knew what was going on and why someone was trying to kill her.

Rebecca awoke in a panic and tried to sit up. Pain ripped through her back and she gasped, causing Collin, who was sitting beside her bed, to jump up.

She grabbed his arm. "That woman! She held me down! She—she—"

"I know, I know. She's gone now."

Sobs racked her and she fell into his embrace. As he held her, she noticed the bruises darkening on her wrists and recalled the horror of being restrained by that monster who'd attacked her.

"You captured her?"

She saw by the grim expression on his face that they hadn't. "Kent is reviewing camera footage with hospital security, but there's no camera with an angle on this room. No one saw anyone coming or going."

The contempt she'd seen in the woman's face flashed through her mind and anger bristled through her. "So she gets away with nearly killing me?"

"She won't, Rebecca. Do you remember what she looked like? What she was wearing?"

Rebecca could never forget her face. "She was wearing scrubs. Her name tag said Mary. She was here when you left. You don't remember seeing her?"

He shook his head. "I guess I wasn't paying that much attention to the staff. I'm sorry. I should have been. I mistakenly thought you would be safe here."

"It's not your fault, Collin. She was a tall, heavyset woman. I tried to fight her, but she pinned me down. I couldn't move. She injected me with something and said by the time anyone found me, it would be too late."

He squeezed her hand. "It wasn't. I found you in time."

She stared up into his green eyes and felt a rush of gratitude for this man. "You came back for me? I thought I was going to die, really going to die this time." She wiped away several tears that rushed down her face. She didn't want Collin to see her cry, but she wasn't sure she could stop it.

"Kent is sending those threatening letters to the lab. I wish you'd given them to him when you first started receiving them."

She should have gone to the police with the letters, but they hadn't been particularly helpful when Missy had disappeared. She'd assumed they wouldn't be any more helpful about anonymous notes. And she hadn't been able to convince herself, truly convince herself, that her suspicions were anything more than suspicion and speculation.

Until now.

Until Missy had shown up at her door two days ago.

Until someone had tried to kill her.

"I should have. I didn't show them to anyone."

"Not even your father? He could have arranged protection for you. Hired you a bodyguard."

"No, I couldn't tell him." Missy had claimed to see Mason Industries on the building where she'd been held, which meant her father might be involved in this. She couldn't trust him. The truth was she didn't know who she could trust anymore. Everyone was a suspect.

"Why not? What's going on, Rebecca?"

"I have a client, a teenaged girl I worked with named Missy, who went missing a few months ago. The police investigated but ultimately listed her as a runaway. But I knew this girl, Collin, and she wouldn't have run away. I worried something terrible had happened to her, that she'd been a victim of foul play or abducted into a human trafficking ring. Foster kids are especially susceptible to traffickers. I started asking questions of all the people she knew. I put up missing posters and set up a Facebook page hoping someone would have information about her they wanted to share. I even started checking the news online for all the surrounding areas in case her body turned up somewhere else, like if she was the victim of a serial killer." She'd felt silly even considering that possibility at the time, but no more.

"Did they find her body?"

"No, but I did find a mention of another missing girl who was found dead. She'd recently given birth and, Collin, she was from right here in Moss Creek. She was a foster kid, just like Missy, who went missing one day. I recognized her name immediately, but I hadn't had much contact with her because her file was transferred to another county not long after I first met her. They found her a hundred miles across the border in Arkansas, and there was no sign anywhere of the baby she'd given birth to."

"What was her cause of death?"

"The medical examiner ruled it as an overdose."

"But you didn't believe that?"

"I didn't. I also was unable to find any trace of what happened to that child. He or she was never entered into the foster care system either here or in Arkansas. I checked with a social worker friend that lives there."

"She might have left it at a safe haven or put it up for a private adoption. Then she felt remorse and OD'd."

"I'm familiar with the adoption process. My cousin adopted her son and it was long and complicated. I realize it's possible this girl had no connection to Missy, but I kept digging and I found other missing girls, all of them pregnant, and none of them had reason to run away from their foster homes. I became convinced I was dealing with some sort of baby-selling ring."

He frowned, obviously unconvinced. It was true she'd had no real evidence of a baby-selling operation—not until Missy confirmed her suspicions. Yet, he reached for her hand and squeezed it, a gesture that gave her comfort and assurance that he believed what she was saying. "Still, you've obviously stumbled onto something. Someone wants you dead. There has to be a reason for that."

She took a deep breath and made a decision. She needed to trust someone and Collin had proven himself today. Besides, he'd been out of the country for the past few months. He was the only person she knew for certain wasn't involved. "There's more," she said and he looked at her. "Two nights ago, Missy reappeared. She showed up at my door. She'd been beaten and terrorized. She confirmed everything I'd suspected. She'd been held hostage and had her baby stolen from her."

His eyes widened. "What? She was here in town?"

"Somehow, she escaped and came to me for help. I've been trying to help her piece together where it was they were held, but she was so panicked that she can't be sure of anything. It can't be far away because she hitchhiked to get here. She doesn't remember being in the car for more than an hour or so."

Collin jumped to his feet. "Where is she now? We have to get her to the police."

"She won't go. She's afraid the police are involved. She claims she saw someone in a law enforcement uniform talking with one of her captors. I don't know who she saw or from what town or county, but she's convinced the police are involved. She was so frightened and I knew I couldn't keep her at my house in case they came looking for her so I hid her out at a motel."

Collin leaned over her, his brow tightening in a way she remembered it did when he was anxious. "Rebecca, what if they followed her here? They know you have her. They could have already gotten to her at the motel. If this is true, they'll do anything to keep her from ruining their operation."

She saw the fear in his eyes and suddenly felt the weight of what she was doing. She'd been too deep in protecting Missy to even think about the consequences of hiding her out. But three attacks in one day had opened her eyes. "I know there's danger, but I can't abandon her. I also can't take the risk that she'll run again if I go to the police before she's ready to talk."

"Kent is right outside questioning the nurses. He's going to want to talk to you about this latest attack, Rebecca. You need to tell him about Missy."

"I can't. Please, Collin, you're the only one I've trusted with this."

He stared at her and she saw his mind running through all the options. "Well, I can't let you do this alone. I don't know who or what she saw, but you can't just assume all police are dirty because of it. We'll talk to her and take her to the police together and try to sort this all out."

"Thank you, Collin. That means a lot to me." Tears pressed at her eyes. It felt so good to not be in this alone any longer.

Collin stood, his expression grim and worried. He leaned over her, placing a kiss on her head. "Try to get some rest. Don't worry, I'll be here making sure you're safe. No one will bother you. I promise."

Yet just as he made that promise, the door swung open and her cousin Janice entered the room, followed by her father. She didn't miss the way he zeroed in on Collin's hand over hers. Collin obviously didn't miss it, either. He took two steps backward and Rebecca found she missed his presence.

Janice leaned over the bed and embraced her. "What are you doing here?" Rebecca asked. "How did you know?"

"Kent called us," her father said. "He told us what happened."

Good ol' Kent. A family friend for years. He'd obviously neglected to mention Collin's presence, given their reactions to seeing him.

"I'm fine," she assured them. "I wasn't badly hurt."

Her statement did nothing to alleviate the concern on Janice's face. "Honey, look at you. What happened?"

She hadn't seen a mirror but she figured she looked as black and blue and beat-up as she felt.

"Who did this?" her father demanded, slicing his eyes at Collin, who stepped farther away from her bed. She didn't care for the distance he'd put between them.

"Do you know why someone attacked you?" Janice asked her as she sat down.

"It's obvious, isn't it?" her father said. "That neighborhood she lives in is dangerous. You should have let me buy you a place in a nicer area." She was used to his comments about her modest home, but she loved her neighborhood and she didn't want his money.

He turned on Collin next. "What are you doing here?"

She rushed to his defense. "It's okay, Dad. He was there when I was attacked."

Her father gasped and turned to her. "He was at your house tonight?"

"No, I meant the first time I was attacked. This afternoon." She glanced at the clock on the wall and realized it was four a.m. "I mean, yesterday afternoon."

They both gaped at her and she realized Kent had obviously not filled them in about the multiple attacks.

"Someone attacked me in the parking lot of the grocery store today. Collin was there." She glanced at him and smiled, true gratitude welling up inside of her. "He saved my life."

Janice leaped to her feet. "Then he's a hero." She rushed over to him and threw her arms around Collin's neck. "Thank you for being there. We all owe you a debt."

"Yes," her father said, his face less grateful than Janice's. The man didn't know how to admit when he was wrong. "Thank you for your assistance, but we'll handle it from here."

Collin's jaw clenched in a way she remembered meant he was holding back from speaking his mind. Her father had always had that effect on him. "I'll give you some time with your family," he said, turning to Rebecca. "I won't be far."

"Will you come back?" she asked, not surprised at all by the look of disbelief from her father.

He gave her a slight nod. "Don't worry. I'll be close by," he promised, and she believed him. She shouldn't after the way he'd left her all those years ago, but something about his demeanor said he was sticking around. She needed to trust in that, at least for now.

"What is he even doing back in town?" her father demanded when Collin was gone from the room. "I thought we were rid of him for good."

Rebecca couldn't believe the contempt in his voice. "His mother died a few months ago. Perhaps you heard. He's in town to sell her house."

"Oh, that's terrible," Janice said, coming to Collin's defense as she returned to Rebecca's side. "His mother was a very nice lady."

Rebecca was thankful for her cousin's support. Even though they lived in a small town, they didn't move in the same circles as Collin's family. They wouldn't have known that Collin had moved her to a facility to care for her several years ago. But Rebecca knew. She'd kept up with Collin's activities through visits with his mother for years and had seen the woman's steady decline. "I know you never cared for him, but he saved my life. He didn't have to jump in and rescue me, but he did. He's a good man."

Her dad had the good sense to look chagrined. She knew he meant well, but she didn't like being treated like a child. She was a grown woman and knew what was best for her.

Janice leaned over and hugged her neck. "We should go. Get some rest. I'll call and check on you later."

"Thank you."

Her father also planted a kiss on her head but held back as Janice left the room. "I realize you've been through something traumatic, Rebecca, but I hope it hasn't clouded your judgment. That Collin boy cannot be trusted."

She couldn't believe his gall—he was still treating her like a child. "He's not a boy any longer, Dad." He was a man now and she couldn't help reliving what it felt like to be in his arms. She pushed away those thoughts. He'd proven he didn't want her when he'd left her after the miscarriage. But she needed him now and he'd already stepped in multiple times to help her. Maybe he would continue to do so.

"Be careful, Rebecca," her father told her as he walked out, but she wondered if he was referring to the attacks on her life today…or to getting involved with Collin again.

Rebecca lay back in the bed. She needed to guard her heart where Collin was concerned. Her father was right about that. But she believed him when he said he would keep her safe and help her navigate through the potential baby-selling ring she'd uncovered.

It felt good not to be on her own and, for the first time in a long while, she actually felt safe.

THREE

Rebecca insisted on being discharged a few hours later. The doctor reluctantly signed her papers but instructed her to rest and take it easy. Collin helped her to his car. He knew she'd feel better after she'd checked in with Missy and gotten the assurance the girl had safely made it through the night. Rebecca was still weak after her ordeal and he hoped she would go home to rest, but he wasn't surprised when she had other plans.

"I want to go by the police station. I want to know if Kent has found any evidence about who attacked me."

He nearly refused and insisted she needed rest. She handled the pain well, but he could see she was hurting. Then he realized it wouldn't matter. She needed to know what was going on. They both did.

They walked into the police station and located Kent.

"Have you found anything that might identify who is attacking me?" she asked him.

He led them into an office and offered them seats, then pulled out a file. "None of the prints we collected have led to anyone yet, but I can tell you there were different prints at your house than on your car."

"So the person who attacked her in the parking lot wasn't the same guy who broke into her house."

"It appears that way. And, of course, the attacker at the hospital was a woman. We haven't been able to pick up a good image of her on the security footage. She kept her face hidden. Obviously she knew where the cameras were located. None of the employees recognized her photo or anyone matching the description you gave. She must have been posing as a hospital employee. We're still looking into how she got access to the drug she injected into your IV. It doesn't look like any is missing from the hospital, so she may have brought it in herself."

He pulled out the letters, still in their evidence bag. "I've had these dusted for prints but the only ones we found were yours from when you were fingerprinted for your court-related duties. We'll keep searching, but so far, we've come up with very little except you

seem to have antagonized a group of people."
He leaned over the desk and gave Rebecca a
hard look. "Is there anything else you can tell
me about what is going on? I need to know
everything."

Collin watched her stare him down without blinking and wondered if she would
change her mind and tell him about Missy.
Kent could help them protect her, but only
if he could be trusted. It was difficult to believe Kent could be involved in something as
underhanded as baby selling, but Collin had
been gone a long time and people's behavior
often surprised him. If Rebecca had a reason not to trust Kent, he had to respect that.

"I've told you everything I know," she said,
and Collin saw disbelief in Kent's face. He
knew she was hiding something…but did he
know because he was aware the girl had escaped her captors, or because he was good at
his job? It wasn't Collin's decision to make.

As he led her outside to his car, he could
sense she was uneasy. He thought it was fear
rearing its head again and tried to reassure
her. "Don't worry. I'll be there with you. I
won't leave you, but you do need to get some
rest."

She sighed, frustrated. "I'm tired of being
told I need to rest. I've been stressing over all

this for too long. I'm ready to find out who is behind it all. I want to know who is trying to kill me, Collin, and who is after Missy. How can I rest without knowing?"

He understood her anxiousness. He was ready to find out who was behind this, too. But she did need her rest.

"You promised you'd protect me, right?"

She touched his arm, her delicate hand sending shivers through him, and he knew he would protect her with his last breath. He may have squandered his opportunity to be with her all those years ago, and maybe after this was all over and Rebecca was out of danger, she would go back to her job with the court and he would take another covert assignment overseas. But for now he couldn't—he wouldn't—let anyone hurt her again. "I know I've let you down in the past, but I won't this time. I will keep you safe, Rebecca."

"Good. Then you need to know what you're getting into. It's time you meet Missy."

They stopped by the store for more groceries and a few supplies for Missy before heading to the motel. Once they were on their way, Collin wasn't the least bit surprised when Rebecca directed him toward the south end of town, across the railroad tracks. She mentioned the name of the motel where she'd hidden Missy and he was surprised she even knew about this part of town. She'd grown up on the other side of the tracks, the better side. Yet, he supposed with her work with the court and foster systems, she probably saw clients who lived in this area a lot.

He checked his mirrors, careful to make certain no one was following them. She was trusting him with this secret and he wasn't going to let her down by leading the bad guys right to her hiding spot.

"Maybe you can convince Missy to go to the police," Rebecca told him. "I can't believe this is happening right here in our town, Collin. This has always been a good place to live."

"Maybe for you it has been, Rebecca, but not for everyone. I grew up on this side of town, remember. I've seen the darker side of Moss Creek."

"I know you're right. I work with these families every day. It's a side of town I never saw when I was growing up."

"How did you get involved in this career? I would have expected you to go to law school or work in your father's manufacturing firm."

"I never wanted that. All I've ever wanted to do was to help people."

"You seem so different than I remember." But she didn't really. It was an image he was recalling of the spoiled rich girl he'd tried to latch on to in order to protect his heart. But in truth her kindness toward others was the thing that had attracted him to her. She'd always been quick to act when someone in school needed supplies or money for field trips. She'd been generous to a fault with not only her money, but also herself. That was the girl he'd fallen in love with all those years ago. Never pretentious or snobby despite her privileged past.

"I can't imagine your father was very pleased with your career choice."

"No, he wasn't. He expected a lot more from me, I suppose, but I get a lot of satisfaction from my job. Most of these kids have no one else looking out for them. I can make a real difference in their lives."

He liked that. He'd seen too many families in need during his time overseas, enough to realize that everyone needed someone to help them. And Rebecca had always had a giving heart. But had it gotten her in over her head this time?

He pulled into the motel's parking lot and stopped in front of the door she instructed. It was more like an old motor lodge, where all the rooms faced the outside. Maybe it had been in a good part of town when it had first been built, but Collin knew this area had been on the downslide since he was a kid and the chipped paint and cracks in the pavement only strengthened his certainty. No one would expect a woman like Rebecca Mason to ever come here. He was with her and he couldn't even believe it.

He gathered up the bags of groceries then scanned the area, looking for a tail, before Rebecca knocked on the door of room fourteen. It edged open and a petite young girl peered out. When she saw it was Rebecca, she swung open the door, but her expression held worry and panic. "Rebecca, what happened to your face?"

She hadn't told Missy about being attacked. It made sense why she hadn't, but Rebecca should have known the girl would see the gash on her forehead and the bruises on her arms and neck. "I'm fine," she insisted, then pushed her back inside.

Collin followed and closed the door as he scanned the room. It was everything he'd expected. A cheap, loud carpet that looked like it was from the seventies and a TV bolted to the dresser. It was cleaner than he'd anticipated, though. He set the bags on a table as the girl's eyes widened in fear at seeing him.

"Who is this?" the girl asked, the pitch of her voice rising. "Who is he? Did he do this to you?"

Rebecca grabbed her arms and held her, trying to calm her. "No, Missy. This is my friend Collin. He's here to help us."

She shook her head and backed away from him. "No, no, no, why did you bring him here? I asked you not to bring the police."

"Collin is not the police. He's just a friend who wants to help us."

He let the sting of the friend comment slide off him. What was she supposed to tell this frightened, traumatized girl? *This is the man who wasn't good enough to provide for me and my baby, but he'll take good care of you?* He'd stick with being called a friend.

And one look at Missy left him little doubt she'd been traumatized. He spotted bruising around her wrists and ankles, probably from restraints, and her face held a pallor of someone who hadn't gotten much sunlight in a while. Plus, the big oozing, stinking fear flowing off her was a dead giveaway of what she'd endured. But if she didn't get to the police soon, or was examined by a doctor, those marks would fade and any evidence of what she'd suffered would disappear with them.

"I won't hurt you," he said in his gentlest voice, holding his hands up in a motion of surrender. He'd have to be careful not to make any sudden moves around her. "I'm here to help."

Rebecca stepped in. "Missy, someone attacked me yesterday in the parking lot of the grocery store. The people who were holding you captive may know you're here. Collin rescued me. He won't let anything happen to either of us."

He saw panic rising in the girl's face. "They know I'm here?"

"No," he said. "If they knew where you were, they would be here by now."

"What—what do I do? I can't let them find me. I can't put you in danger."

"We need to get you to the authorities," Collin said as terror filled her young face.

"No cops," she said, her hands trembling at the mere mention.

He didn't know what exactly she'd seen, but her fear of the police was unwavering. "Then we at least need to get you checked out by a doctor."

Again, she resisted. "No! No doctors. They'll

know and come take me back. The doctors and police are working together."

He saw what Rebecca meant about her being too afraid to go to the police, but she couldn't stay holed up in this room forever and she needed to share her ordeal with someone with the power to investigate. "How about the FBI then? Kidnapping is a federal offense and from what Rebecca has told me, this ring seems to be operating across state lines. It makes more sense for a baby-selling ring to be part of a bigger network. They wouldn't take the women from the same town where they sell the children."

"That's true," Rebecca said. "I hadn't thought about that." She turned to Missy. "Would you be willing to go to the FBI?"

She folded her arms against herself in a protective manner and looked at them both like she was getting ready to bolt, but she finally nodded her consent to talk with the FBI.

Collin pulled up a chair and motioned for Missy to sit down. "Why don't we try to figure out where you were being held?"

Missy sat on the edge of the bed and Rebecca took the spot next to her.

"Let's start with something easy," he said. "Do you recall anything about the place they were keeping you?"

"It was a large basement area. We were underground for sure because I had to go up the stairs to get outside when I escaped. I ran into the woods and hid. I heard men searching for me but I also heard a highway so I ran toward that sound."

"Did you see any road signs or anything that might tell us where you were?"

"I saw a sign painted on the side of the building. It said Mason Industries."

He was shocked to hear that. He looked at Rebecca and saw tears pooling in her eyes. No wonder she had questions about her father's involvement. But Collin was certain no matter what Bob Mason was involved in, he would never agree to anything that placed a target on his only daughter's back. However, it was possible he'd gotten into business with people who didn't care about Rebecca's safety as much as he did.

"What did you do next?" he asked, turning back to Missy.

"I ran toward the highway and I flagged down a big rig. He gave me a ride to a truck stop on the outskirts of Moss Creek. I walked to Rebecca's house from there."

"And you don't remember how long you were driving?"

"No, I must have dozed off because the

driver had to wake me when we arrived. I don't know how long I slept."

"Do you remember the man's name or what trucking company was on the side of the truck?"

She shook her head, looking defeated. "I can't remember. I was just so scared."

The way she clung to Rebecca told him her fear was real, and so was their bond. She was fortunate to have someone like Rebecca in her life, especially knowing that many kids in the foster care system had no one. "What about the police?" he asked her. "You told Rebecca you saw the police talking to your kidnappers."

She nodded and scooted closer to Rebecca on the bed.

"Did you recognize the man you saw? Was he wearing a uniform? How did you know he was the police?"

"He was wearing a uniform like one that a deputy wore when he came to our school one time when I was younger. He had a gun and one of those starlike badges that said 'deputy sheriff' on it."

"Had you ever seen him before?"

She shook her head. "No. He looked at me, though. He stared right at me and then talked about me like I wasn't even there. Like I was an animal in a cage. He said I would make fine product because of my blond hair and blue eyes."

So they were holding the girls to use them again. He would have to remind Rebecca to get a copy of the photo of the dead girl and show it to Missy to see if she recognized her. If they were keeping these girls, then why had that one been found dead of an apparent overdose? Was she a victim of this ring of kidnappers or simply a runaway who had overdosed with no connection at all? It would also tell him for certain what kind of people they were dealing with. They had already tried to kill Rebecca. Were they the type who didn't care how high the body count went?

Rebecca hugged her tight. "Thank you, Missy. I'm sorry we had to ask these questions. Collin and I are going to go make the arrangements to meet with the FBI, but you'll be safe here as long as you stay inside. If you need anything, call me. You have the number."

Collin was impressed with how gentle and understanding Rebecca was with the girl and she could see how important Rebecca's opinion was to her.

They left, Rebecca ensuring that Missy

locked the door before they walked to the car. "What did you think?" she asked him.

He was still trying to process it all but his overriding thoughts were for Rebecca's safety. "She's obviously been through something traumatic and I can see she's reluctant to go to the police. Where's the closest FBI office?"

"I'm not sure. Probably in Jackson. That's at least ninety miles away."

"You said earlier you've been collecting evidence on Missy's abduction?"

"Yes, as well as three other girls that went missing in the past year from the foster care system. As far as I can tell, they had nothing else in common except that they were all pregnant and their foster families, teachers and case workers didn't believe they were the type to run away. It's only notes of people I've talked to as well as the newspaper articles I found. They didn't lead me anywhere, but when the threats started showing up, I got scared and printed off a hard copy just in case I needed it and hid it at my house. I felt silly at the time. But, if Kent has been through my house, don't you think he found that?"

"They were looking for evidence of a break-in, not a stash of secret documents. Besides, I think he would have mentioned it."

"Unless he's involved with the kidnappers."

Suspicion clouded her expression and he saw she was struggling with who to trust, but he wasn't ready to write off Kent as one of the bad guys until Missy could give them more information about who or what she saw. "For now, I'm giving him the benefit of the doubt. It's difficult for me to believe that someone I've known since fourth grade could change so much. Let's go get your files then get back to Missy. I'd like to know if she recognizes any of these other missing girls. I'll also call the FBI and find out who we need to contact and when we can come in."

They got into the car and Collin drove to her house. He felt her stiffen when he pulled into the driveway. She'd been through so much and being attacked in her own home had to be devastating.

He thought the police would have locked up after they left last night, but as he got out of the car, he saw that the front door was open. He motioned for her to wait as he approached the door and peered inside. Furniture was overturned and papers were scattered everywhere, as if someone had been searching for something. It hadn't been that way last night. He also noted the lock on the door was busted.

She gasped but stayed behind him as he checked the house. The bedroom was also in a worse state than it had been last night after her attack. When he entered the room, her dresser drawers were pulled open and clothes were scattered. Someone had been searching for something here. Her notes? Or a clue as to where she was hiding Missy?

She pushed through the mess to the other side of the bed then gasped and placed her hands over her mouth. Her nightstand was overturned and only pieces of tape remained stuck to the bottom.

"It's gone," she said. "I taped it to the bottom of my nightstand. All my notes are gone."

It seemed it hadn't been silly of her to hide those papers, only unnecessary. He checked the rest of the house but no one was inside. They'd found what they'd come for. They knew she was connecting the dots about the missing girls. But did they also know Missy had run to her after escaping?

Kent hadn't mentioned anything about the inside of her house being ransacked and he doubted it was police procedure to do this much searching on a victim's home. He pulled out his phone and dialed Kent's number.

"Did you search Rebecca's entire house?"

"I cleared it for intruders, if that's what you mean."

"Her place has been ransacked. Overturned furniture, drawers pulled out and clothes scattered."

Kent sucked in a breath. "That wasn't us and it wasn't like that when we were there. Her house was in order when we left it. I'll send a team over there right away."

"Do you believe him?" Rebecca asked.

That was the kicker. He didn't know what to believe. It made no sense that someone would come back to her house to search for those papers after breaking in to write the threat on her wall. If they knew about them, why hadn't they taken them when they broke in previously? Unless...

"You said you printed off a copy of everything you've collected? Do you still have it saved on your laptop?"

"Yes, but it's in my car at the impound lot."

Collin pulled out his phone again and sent Kent a text message. "I'm asking Kent to check your car to see if your laptop is still inside. Someone could have taken it, found the information you had on it and assumed you printed it out. That's the only thing that makes sense."

"So they know all the information I've gathered and everyone I've spoken with."

His phone dinged with a message and his gut clenched as Kent confirmed what he'd suspected. Her car had been inventoried as part of gathering evidence at the crime scene, but her laptop was not there. Was this the work of Missy's dirty cop?

"You're sure the laptop was in your car?"

She nodded. "I'm positive. Why?"

"It was never inventoried as part of the evidence. It's gone." He took her arm. "We should go. You can recount whatever you remember to the FBI and they can pick up the trail you started."

The sooner they got Missy out of town and to the FBI, the better off they were going to be. If anything happened to her—if anything happened to either of them, before they could get to the FBI to tell their story—the ring would have succeeded in tying up their loose ends and could continue on unscathed.

He opened the passenger door for Rebecca but before she got in, from the corner of his eye, he spotted a car approaching them, slowly. The window lowered and the barrel of a gun poked out.

His instincts kicked in and he grabbed Rebecca and threw her to the ground behind the car as gunshots rang out, spraying his car with bullets.

Rebecca screamed as Collin threw her to the ground, but her heart hammered when he covered her with his body as shots rang out. Her pulse roared in her ears, and over the gunfire and screeching of tires, all she heard was the rapid beating of her heart.

When the car was gone, he released her. "Are you okay?" Collin asked, grabbing her arms and helping her up. "Are you hit?"

She couldn't even catch her breath but she managed to shake her head. "I—I'm okay."

He pulled out his phone and called the police. The car was long gone but the threat was very real. Someone was determined to kill Rebecca. Had they been hiding as they waited for them to return to her house? Or had they followed them here from the motel?

She gasped, yanked out her phone and dialed the motel. Relief rushed through her when Missy answered.

"Are you okay?" Rebecca asked her, the high-pitched sound of her voice seeming frantic even to her own ears.

"I'm fine. Why? What happened?"

She forced herself to breathe and keep her

voice steady before she responded. "Nothing, nothing. I was only checking on you."

But Missy wasn't dumb. "I can tell by your voice something is wrong, Rebecca. What is it? Am I in danger?"

"No. Someone shot at us at my house, but you're safe. If they knew where you were, they would be there by now. Keep the door locked and the curtains drawn and don't answer the door for anyone."

She made Missy promise and then ended the call, but once she hung up, Rebecca dropped the phone and sobbed into her hands as the weight of what was happening overwhelmed her. Someone had shot at her! It wasn't right that she had to endure this. She was trying to do the right thing and it wasn't fair the bad guys kept coming after her. Where was God in all this? Where was the truth?

Collin rushed to her, his eyes searching hers as he pulled her to him and she laid her head on his shoulder. It was strong and comforting and seemed as if it could handle the weight of the world.

"Missy is okay. How did they know we were here?" she asked him. "Did they follow us?"

"I don't think so. I didn't notice anyone following us and I was watching."

She spotted several of her neighbors peeking through curtains and opening their doors to see what all the commotion was about. Now that the shots were over, curiosity would get the best of everyone and they would want to know what had happened. In the distance, the sound of sirens whirled toward them.

When the first police car arrived, Collin told them what had happened. She was amazed at how well he was handling this situation. She was a wreck, shaking and scared, but he seemed unfazed. He'd reacted on instinct and drive, and it broke her heart to imagine he'd seen a lot of gunfire in his time in the army. But even those thoughts brought up new feelings of anger. He'd only joined the army to get away from her. She had to stop being so dependent on him. All she was doing was opening her heart to someone she knew would break it again.

She walked toward him as a deputy was asking questions and taking down notes. "Did you get a look at the car or the shooter?"

"The car was tan and a four-door. I couldn't make out the tag number. The shooter was sitting in the back seat. I didn't get a look at the driver."

The deputy glanced her way. "We'll need to get your statement as well."

She took a deep breath and recounted what she recalled about the car. It wasn't much. She'd seen it approaching but then Collin had reacted and shielded her.

"Maybe we'll be fortunate and find security footage of the car leaving the neighborhood."

Several more cruisers arrived and they taped off the area around her driveway, then started questioning those who'd converged in the street. Collin stayed beside Rebecca, his arm around her. Despite her earlier determination to not rely so much on him, she placed her head on his shoulder as tears slipped through. She couldn't hold them back. Too much was happening and it felt like her world was being shaken. She didn't even have time to breathe, much less figure out what was happening.

"It's going to be okay," Collin whispered, tightening his grip on her.

"I'm just ready for it to stop." And she could probably make it stop by handing over Missy to the baby-selling ring, but she wouldn't. No matter what happened to her, she wouldn't give up on Missy or on taking down the people who seemed to think it was okay to kidnap women like Missy and steal their babies. She glanced up at Collin, remembering their child and how devastating it had been to lose the baby. Miscarrying was something she wouldn't wish on her worst enemy, but snatching a child from its mother's arms... She shuddered at the thought.

Kent arrived on the scene and Collin hurried to him. "Where were you? I thought you were on your way."

"I got here as soon as I could. I sent a cruiser. I heard the call over the radio. Shots fired. What happened?"

"Someone shot up my car and nearly shot us."

Kent moved toward Rebecca. "Are you okay?"

"I'm fine. I'm fortunate Collin was here with me." She didn't want to believe the worst about him, but he had known they were at her house. Had he arranged for the shooting? He was the only one who'd known they were there. She glanced at Collin as he pulled his hands through his hair. She recognized that tell of frustration, too. He had to be asking himself the same questions about Kent that she was.

"We will interview your neighbors. Maybe one of them saw something more. Possibly, it's the same people and they were watching and waiting for you to come home. Either way, once again, your house is a crime scene, Rebecca. You can't stay here. Do you have somewhere you can go?"

Tears filled her eyes that her home had been broken into yet another time. Would she ever consider it home again without feeling violated? She didn't know, but Kent was right. Even if it wasn't currently a crime scene, she couldn't see staying here for now. It was time to make other arrangements. "I can go to my cousin Janice's house. She has a spare bedroom." And maybe hugging her cousin's baby for a few hours would give her some comfort.

Collin nodded. "I'll call us a cab then drop you off at your cousin's house. I need to get a rental since my car is now undrivable." He motioned toward his car and she turned to see his sedan riddled with bullet holes.

Kent nodded. "I'll phone you when we know something more about the shooting."

When the cab arrived, she gave her cousin's address, hoping she wasn't imposing too much on Janice and her husband, David. Truthfully, she would rather stay with Collin—she would feel safer—but that wasn't a good idea. She couldn't take it if she fell for Collin all over again and he left her just when she needed him. She may trust him to keep her safe but she couldn't—she wouldn't—trust him with her heart.

Collin asked the cabdriver to wait while he got out, then he walked Rebecca to the door of her cousin's house. He wasn't surprised to find she lived in an upscale neighborhood. Rebecca's father had taken in Janice as a young child after her mother's death and she was probably used to the same privileged life that Rebecca had been raised in.

He spotted Janice pull back the curtain and then open the door before they even reached it. She ran out to greet them, a worried look on her face as she threw her arms around her cousin. "Rebecca, where have you been? Your father has been blowing up my phone for the past hour trying to see if I'd heard from you. He called the hospital and discovered you were released. You haven't answered any of our texts or phone calls."

"I guess my phone was on silent," she said. "I'm fine. We've been at the police station talking with the detective in charge of my case."

He was surprised that was all she said. She probably didn't want to worry her cousin, but she would certainly find out what happened at the house soon enough.

"Have they found out who is doing this to you?" Janice asked.

"Not yet, but something else has happened. I can't go back to my house. I was hoping I could stay with you and David."

"Of course you can. Come on inside and tell me what happened." She walked Rebecca into the house as Collin followed behind and closed the door. He would only stay a moment to check out the security of the house and make certain Rebecca was safe.

He took a moment to notice the high-priced furnishings and rugs, but Rebecca distracted him when she squealed then rushed into the living room. He followed her just in time to see her swoop up a child from a playpen.

"Hello, Matthew," she said, giving the baby in her arms kisses on his chubby cheeks as he giggled. She turned to Collin and for the first time in a very long time, he saw happiness spread across her face. He liked it.

"Collin, this is Matthew."

He looked at the baby and saw a patch of blond hair, pale skin and blue eyes. He looked to be about a year old although Collin was no expert on babies.

Janice laughed, put her hand on Collin's

arm and led him toward the sofa. "She always does that. She'll be occupied for a while. Won't you sit, Collin?" He sat and Janice took the spot beside him. "Rebecca told me about your mother. I'm very sorry for your loss."

"Thank you." He was grateful for her civility. She'd never been openly hostile toward Collin, but then again she'd been barely a teenager when he and Rebecca had eloped.

"How long are you planning on being back in town?"

His intention had been to get in and out as quickly as possible, but he knew he'd only been lying to himself. If he hadn't wanted to be here, he could have hired someone to close up his mother's house. He'd wanted to see Rebecca, hoped to accidentally bump into her again just to get a glimpse of how her life was. It would have made him happy to know she had a good life. But he'd never expected to find her in danger. He glanced at Rebecca. She changed everything. "I'm not sure yet."

The baby started crying and Janice stood to take him, but Rebecca waved her away. "He probably just needs to be changed," she said. "I'll take care of it."

She carried him from the room and disappeared upstairs.

"It must be strange to see Rebecca again after all this time," Janice said once she was gone.

Strange was an understatement. "It is."

"Twelve years is a long time. Tell me something about yourself. Did you ever get married?"

He stared at her, looking for some sort of angle in her eyes, then remembered Rebecca hadn't told anyone about their marriage or the child they'd lost. "I did once," he admitted. "It didn't work out." It didn't work out because he'd been a scared boy pretending to be a man and he'd let down the woman he loved.

"I'm sorry to hear that. Marriage is wonderful. David, my husband, and I have been together for eight years. Do you have any kids?"

He shook his head. That was another dream that hadn't worked out for him and Rebecca. "No kids. Is Matthew your only child?"

"Yes, he is, but we'd love to have more. Rebecca's always loved kids. I thought by now she would have gotten married and had a house full, but she's never been that interested in anyone..." She gave him a sideways glance and left off the words *except you*.

Her family couldn't possibly understand since they didn't know she was legally married to Collin, but it broke his heart to hear how alone she'd been for the past twelve years. He'd wished so much more for her than a life lived without love.

A smiling Rebecca returned with Matthew in her arms. "He's all clean and dry. I appreciate you letting me stay here. I hope David won't mind."

"Of course he wouldn't mind, but he's out of town for the next several days."

Rebecca stopped and placed the baby back into his playpen. "Wait, David's not home?"

"Well, no, but it's fine. We'll have a good old-fashioned girls' night." She stood and took Rebecca's arm. "Now, tell me what is happening with you. Why does someone want to hurt you?"

Rebecca glanced at him before sitting her cousin down and telling her almost the whole story. Collin noted that she omitted the fact that she was hiding Missy out at the motel.

Janice's face was full of horror as Rebecca told her about the men and the woman who'd attacked her. "Rebecca, you have to stop this. Do whatever they want so they'll leave you alone."

Janice was right, but the Rebecca he knew would never give up on someone. He saw determination flash through her eyes. "I can't.

I won't. I can't let them get away with hurting girls like this."

"But they'll kill you, Rebecca."

"I won't let that happen," Collin assured them both.

Rebecca's eyes shone with gratitude but he still saw concern on Janice's face.

"No! Rebecca, you're not the police. You shouldn't be putting yourself in danger this way. Think about your father and how he would feel if something happened to you. What about me, or Matthew? I don't want him to grow up without his aunt."

Rebecca pulled her into a hug. "I'll be fine, Janice, but I can't just walk away from this. Too many lives are at risk." She pulled away from her cousin. "And I don't think I should stay here after all. I don't want to put you and Matthew in jeopardy."

"Don't be silly. We're fine. We have a security system."

"No, it's not right to put you and Matthew in that kind of danger." She turned to Collin. "It would probably be better if I stayed at a hotel."

He couldn't argue with that decision. He could protect her better if he was closer and he could do that if she was in a hotel. "I think that would be for the best," he told her.

"Rebecca, no!" Janice grabbed her arm. "I won't let you do this."

Rebecca hugged her again. "I'm sorry. I shouldn't have come. I won't drag you and your family down with me."

She turned to Collin and he led her outside as Janice followed them to the door.

"Are you sure you want to do this?" he asked as they headed for the cab.

She shook her head as she stared back at her cousin. "No, but it's what I need to do."

He admired her bravery and determination so much. That was the Rebecca he knew, although she'd never had to face the kind of danger she was in now. As she slid into the back of the cab, Collin vowed he would keep her safe.

FOUR

Anxiety poured out of Rebecca as they rode to a hotel. So many thoughts rushed through her mind. How were they going to keep Missy safe? Who were they even fighting against and how could they ever win?

Collin reached for her hand and squeezed it, then gave her a wink and a reassuring smile. "Everything is going to be okay," he told her in a way that made her really believe him. It was a moment like this that she wished she could slide across the seat, lean into him, rest her head against his shoulder and take comfort in his reassuring words. But she hesitated. She'd clung to him in a moment of panic and fear before, but it seemed inappropriate to do so when she wasn't hysterical. That part of their relationship had ended long ago. He'd packed up, left her and never looked back, never contacted her or tried to work out their problems.

She'd missed him so much and he probably hadn't even thought about her in the past twelve years. She'd found a way to live without him, but her life had been empty and incomplete without this man by her side. She'd lost her one chance at love when she'd lost Collin and she regretted every single day how things had happened between them.

She was staring at him, watching the way his chin twitched as his eyes scanned the area, when she noticed a car approaching them as they entered an intersection. It wasn't slowing down.

"Car!" she screamed as it rammed into the back passenger side of the cab, just missing hitting Collin. The driver swerved and the car spun out of control. Collin's hand slipped from hers and she went tumbling as the car flipped. Her seat belt locked and the final impact threw her forward, then backward. When it stopped, the car was on its side.

Rebecca fought to regain her equilibrium after the impact. She spotted Collin a few inches from her, moving slowly, just as she was. The cabbie groaned then unbuckled.

"Are you both all right?" he asked.

"I think so," Rebecca replied.

"I'm okay, too," Collin responded but he sounded as jarred as she was.

The driver crawled out of the car, and Rebecca looked out the back window and spotted the other driver approaching. Her head was still spinning but she thought she saw the man pull a mask over his face then take out a gun. She tried to yell a warning, but the words wouldn't come. She reached for Collin, to try to tell him, but it was too late. The masked man fired two shots and the cabbie went down.

Collin grabbed her arm and pulled her from the car. "Run!" he shouted at her and Rebecca took off, only vaguely aware of Collin behind her as a round of gunfire sounded in her ears. When she slowed or tried to stop, he pushed her along, forcing her not to give up. Bullets ricocheted around her and it was inconceivable that one didn't hit her.

They ran into the park and across the Moss Creek walkway before reaching the part of town called Medical Row, which was a group of buildings that surrounded the hospital.

Collin grabbed her arm, slowing her to a brisk walk. "We lost him in the park." Rebecca felt the tension flowing off of him. He was on high alert and ready to take on anyone who tried to get in their way. But what match were they for armed men?

She heard the noise of sirens behind them. Had they captured the man who'd rammed into them then started shooting? Was the cabbie dead? And how had the people after her managed once again to know exactly where they would be for an attack?

She was out of breath when they reached the hospital and entered the ER through the ambulance bay. No one was at the desk so they walked through. She'd seen this ER bustling, but now it was quiet and empty.

Collin nodded toward an empty medical cart. "Grab some gauze and tape," he told her, and only then did she notice how pale he was and how there was blood smeared on his fingers where he was holding his left arm.

"You're hurt."

"It's just a graze. He hit me as we were running off." He motioned toward the cart. "See if they have some."

"You need a doctor." She started to search for someone but he stopped her.

"The people that are after us don't care about collateral damage, Rebecca. The cabdriver is dead. They won't hesitate to kill any of these people here. We don't have time to stop for paperwork and updated insurance information. All I need is to stop the bleeding and I'll be fine."

The frown lines on his face were deep. She didn't know if it was from pain or worry or both, but she hurried toward the cart and found gauze, tape and antiseptic. "Got it." The sound of footsteps caught her attention. "Someone's coming." She grabbed his arm and led him through a door into the main part of the hospital. He was dragging now and leaning more on her, and Rebecca knew she had to find somewhere to dress his wounds fast.

She saw a patient room with no name and pushed open the door. The room was dark and empty, just what they needed.

Collin flicked on the bedside lamp, sat on the bed, removed his jacket and raised his shirt, exposing the wound in the back of his arm.

"Have you ever cleaned a gunshot wound?" he asked her and once again she was reminded of all he must have seen and done in the years since they'd been apart.

She shook her head. This was a first for her. He reached for her hand and gave her a slight, pain-riddled smile. "It's okay. I'll walk you through it. It's only a flesh wound."

"It's bleeding a lot, Collin."

"That's just because we've been running."

He walked her through cleaning the wound and taping it up. As she finished, she couldn't help but notice the older, faded scars on his back.

"You've been wounded before."

She fingered one and felt him shudder beneath her touch. "Once or twice."

A tear rolled from her eye as she realized all he'd been through without her. War. Battles. Loneliness.

She stood in front of him, her hand grazing his cheek as he removed his shirt and looked up at her. All he'd endured seemed to shine in his eyes. He'd been broken and battered, but Collin—her Collin—was still there behind the dark green that stared back at her. "Sometimes you're just like the man I knew and sometimes you seem like someone completely different."

His eyes seemed to search her, digging right through her barriers to the regrets of her soul. "It's been a long time. I suppose we've both changed."

She tucked a stray curl behind his ear and he gave a sigh. His hands went around her and he pulled her toward him. He was going to kiss her and if the flutter in her stomach was any indication, she was going to let him.

"Not again!" an exasperated voice from the

doorway said. "Don't you kids have anything better to do than sneak into hospital rooms and—" The main lights flickered on and the woman in scrubs stopped.

Rebecca suddenly realized what they must look like to her.

"Aren't you two a little old for this?" she asked with a smirk on her face.

Collin grabbed Rebecca's hand. "Sorry," he said as he pulled her out of the room behind him and hurried down the corridor.

Giggles escaped her as they hurried through the hospital searching for an exit. Collin was grinning, too, at being mistaken for a couple of teenagers.

"Apparently, they have a problem with kids sneaking in and making out," he said. "If I'd known that was an option when we were teenagers, we would have definitely done it."

She laughed at his humor and he slid his arm easily over her shoulder the way he used to. For a moment, they were those kids again. But the lightheartedness of the moment evaporated once they hit the mugginess of the afternoon air.

He pulled his arm away and went on high alert once again, his smile replaced by the frown lines on his forehead. "We're too exposed out on the street. We should find a place to stay." He motioned toward a hotel that was visible just a block away. "I say we check in there and lay low for a while."

As he took her hand and led her down the street, Rebecca couldn't help but compare the boy she'd known to the man who was with her. She'd loved Collin with all her heart and she hated to think what he'd had to go through these past twelve years, but she was glad for it because she needed the man Collin was now to keep her and Missy safe.

He couldn't believe he'd almost kissed her! What had he been thinking going down that road again? He could only chalk it up to excessive blood loss and the adrenaline pumping through his veins. That and the sweet scent of her shampoo.

He'd seen horror in her face at what he'd been through, but it had made him the man he was today, the man who could protect her like he never could have before. He didn't regret joining the army or any of his missions. He didn't even regret breaking orders and rushing in with his team to save those in the American embassy three months ago. The only regrets he had were for the people he'd lost. He should have been better.

He glanced at Rebecca as she checked them

into the hotel. He had to do better for her, too. He couldn't let her down the way he had all those years ago. He'd promised to take care of her, but he couldn't and she'd lost the baby and her faith in him because of it.

She approached him with two key cards. "I got us adjoining rooms. I used a prepaid debit card I'd gotten for Missy so no one should be able to trace us here."

"Good thinking," he said, hating the fact that she had to think about details like that... and that he hadn't thought of it himself. He was supposed to be looking out for her, but now—he grimaced at the pain in his arm— it seemed like it was the other way around.

They rode the elevator to the third floor then he cleared both rooms and locked the doors behind them, making sure all the locks were set. He closed the drapes before switching on the lamp in her room. It was starting to get dark outside and he could already see the weariness on Rebecca's face.

"You should lie down," he told her. "Time to take one of those pain pills the doctor gave you at the hospital and try to get some rest."

"What about you?"

"I'll keep watch."

"You need rest, too. You lost a lot of blood."

He shook his head. "I'll be fine. I've gone

days without sleep while on missions. I'm used to it."

"Collin, I'm glad you're here with me. I don't know what I would have done if you hadn't swooped in to rescue me."

He smiled. He'd never swooped in his life, but he appreciated the sentiment. Besides, he owed her. "It's the least I can do for you, Rebecca, after the way I let you down."

"What do you mean, the way you let me down?"

"When we were together. I promised to take care of you, but I—I couldn't. I'm sorry about that."

She stood and walked to him. She touched his arm softly, sending shivers through him. "You never let me down, Collin. I was the one who failed you. I failed us both."

He couldn't believe what she was saying. "How did you ever let me down?"

"By being what I am—a spoiled little rich girl. If I had taken better care of myself…if I hadn't been so demanding—"

"You were never demanding." In fact, she'd been too agreeable to living in the squalor of all he could afford back then. It had been a far cry from the mansion where she grew up. "You don't strike me as being a spoiled little rich girl anymore. You've built a life for yourself. You're strong and brave and you should be proud of yourself. I am." He was the one who'd let her down and she was trying to apologize to him. "You're tired. Get some rest. No one will bother you. I promise."

"Thank you, Collin." She whispered the words as she crawled onto the bed and drifted off to sleep.

He watched her. He'd been a terrible husband and provider, but he was a good protector. He'd garnered the skills he needed to keep her safe and even though he would never be able to call her his again, he vowed he would protect her.

He peeked through the curtains to the street below. The streetlights had come on, illuminating the area, but there was little traffic. He saw nothing that concerned him. Yet. But whoever was after Rebecca would be back. They'd found her several times but this last attack baffled him the most. How had they known where and when they were headed, or that they had taken a cab? Had they been watching when they left Rebecca's house? Were they tracking them somehow? Through their cell phones? Or was Missy right and someone on the force was involved with the ring? The house had been surrounded by police when the cab arrived.

Only two people had known where they were going and now one of them was dead. He'd seen the driver's wound and knew from experience he wasn't getting back up. Kent was the only other person who'd known they were going to Janice's house. They hadn't told anyone else.

Kent.

Had his old friend betrayed them to the ring?

His cell phone rang and he glanced at the caller ID.

He pressed the answer button. "Hello, Kent."

"Collin! Where are you? What happened? We found the cab you left in. The driver's dead."

"Someone ambushed us as we were leaving Rebecca's cousin's house."

"I know. I'm at the scene now. Where are you? I'll come and get you."

"No. We're safe for now." He hated believing his old friend was untrustworthy, but he wasn't going to risk their lives again by taking a chance and telling him where they were, either.

He heard the exasperation in Kent's tone. "Collin, I have a dead man here. I need you and Rebecca to come in and give me a statement. I know she knows what's going on. It's time she tells me the truth."

The truth?

He glanced at her, already sleeping on the bed. She was the most truthful person he'd ever known and she had a right to be cautious. His experience with terrorists had taught him that just because someone raised the white flag didn't mean they were trustworthy.

But Kent did deserve the truth. "She doesn't trust you, Kent."

Silence filled the other side of the line, then came his stunned response. "What?'

"She doesn't trust you and neither do I. Too many things have happened that make us both suspicious of the sheriff's office."

"You think I'm dirty? I've known you both since we were kids. How could you think that about me?"

"People change." He certainly had. He'd seen too much, especially during his time as a covert operative. Secrets and lies were facts of life. "How did the shooters know we were at Rebecca's house? Or that we'd taken a cab? Only you knew that."

"I would never do anything to hurt Rebecca. I would never—"

"Look, Kent, right now my goal is just to keep her safe," Collin said, interrupting his

I'm-the-good-guy spiel. He ended the call and turned off the phone so they couldn't track it then picked up Rebecca's and shut it off as well. She'd already spoken to Missy earlier. She could turn it on again briefly tomorrow to see if Missy called during the night.

Then he remembered he needed to contact someone with the FBI to make arrangements. He turned his phone back on long enough to look up a phone number—an old ranger buddy who'd married an FBI agent a few years back and was local. He remembered the connection because they'd both grown up in small towns in Mississippi only to meet thousands of miles away in another part of the world. He jotted down the number then shut off his phone again and grabbed the hotel line, hoping his old friend Josh Adams would remember and help him.

He did remember Collin and listened as he explained what was going on. "I'm out of the state right now," he said, "but my wife is still with the FBI. In fact, she heads up a human-trafficking task force, so I know she'll want to hear what you have to say. I'll give her your number and have her call you."

He gave Josh his cell phone number as well as the number for the hotel room then thanked him and hung up. It felt good to have a contact, someone who knew they were fighting for their lives here. He hoped she would call soon.

He worked out the scenario of the events in his mind as he stood watch. The ring wasn't necessarily connected to his hometown, but there had to be a presence close by that Missy had escaped from. An empty warehouse with Mason Industries painted on the side. He'd read that Rebecca's father had moved much of his manufacturing operations out of the country, where employee wages were lower, but the last he recalled he'd had vast holdings across several states. The empty warehouse could be any one of a number of buildings.

He shuddered just thinking about the kind of evil that would perpetuate such an idea as to steal a child from one woman and sell it to another. He'd seen that kind of evil and callousness before, but that had been overseas in countries where women were little more than baby makers. This was his country, his state, his very hometown where this kind of malice was operating. It was monstrous.

He glanced up at the night sky through the curtain and wondered not for the first time where God was in all of this. Had He abandoned them all? Collin deserved what he got. He'd let too many people down with his failures. But Rebecca didn't deserve this. She was good and pure and innocent, and she'd suffered unbearably all because she'd chosen to place her trust in him.

The sun was up when Rebecca awoke. Her muscles were stiff but she was relatively pain-free, something she hadn't felt in two days.

She heard voices and sat up, scanning the room. She didn't see Collin. She walked toward the door to the adjoining room and the sounds increased. He'd pulled it shut but not all the way, so they could still communicate.

Suddenly, the door opened and he appeared, holding a tray full of food.

"What's going on?"

"I ordered us breakfast."

He set the tray on the table and she took a chair, her stomach growling at the scent of scrambled eggs and freshly fried bacon.

"It smells delicious. I'm starving."

He poured himself a cup of coffee, which surprised her. He hadn't drunk the stuff when they were together, but it wasn't the only thing about him that was different. His morning stubble was fuller and darker, and his hair was curlier. She'd seen him run his hands through it several times and thought that probably accounted for the curls. He was bigger, fuller, a man instead of a boy, yet she still saw the face of the kid who'd stolen her heart.

She dug into her eggs and tried to tromp those memories away. The things she'd felt for Collin once were shadows, figments of a past that wasn't nearly as rosy as she remembered it. He'd broken her heart and proven himself untrustworthy. She could never take that risk again. Why then did she instinctively trust him so much?

"So what is our plan?" she asked him.

"I called an old friend last night. His wife is an FBI agent. Once I hear back from her, we'll set up a meeting so she can interview Missy and hear about the evidence you collected."

She sighed. "Maybe I should have just taken it to Kent to begin with. Maybe none of this would have happened."

"I don't know. Maybe."

He took a swig of his coffee but she saw doubt in his eyes that he tried to hide with the coffee mug.

"Now *you* don't trust him? Why?"

He grimaced. "I don't have a reason, just a gut feeling. I was thinking about it last night and he was the only one who knew where we were headed. How could someone know how to target us unless they knew where we were and which direction we were going?"

She hadn't thought about that, but it made sense. Kent had been the one to ask her where she would be staying and he'd seen them drive away in the cab. Still, they'd known Kent Morris all their lives. But Missy was terrified of cops and Rebecca's gut had told her to hold back what she knew about the kidnapped girl's reappearance. Would Kent really have a total stranger killed? But if he was cold enough to be involved in kidnapping girls and stealing their children, what was murder?

"So we're not trusting Kent, right?"

"Right. I say we lay low until we hear back from the FBI. Once we do, we'll grab Missy and get out of town. I don't want to give anyone else the opportunity to target you." He pulled out his phone and powered it up. "I'm ordering a rental car, and I'll need to stop by my mom's house to pick up something."

She pushed away her food, her stomach suddenly churning with anxiety. They were effectively on the run from everyone she'd ever known, unable to know who to trust and who not to trust, including her own family.

She longed for nothing more than to place her faith in God and know that everything was going to work out. She had once, but that had been a long time ago, back before she'd lost both Collin and her baby. Since that time, she'd gone through the motions, going to church and singing, but it was all surface. She had no faith in the Lord to help her. She'd been hurt too many times to believe the Lord was on her side.

She reached for her phone and saw it was turned off. Collin quickly explained why and his reasoning made sense to her.

"Okay if I see if Missy has called?"

"Sure, but make it brief. We don't need Kent and the locals tracking us down before we can reach the FBI."

She powered up her phone and noticed she had several missed calls and multiple text messages. Many of them were from Kent asking where they were and wondering if they were safe. Others were from family and friends who'd heard about the drive-by shooting and were checking up on her. But one message stood out, sent just an hour ago from her father.

Come to the hospital. Janice was attacked at her home this morning.

FIVE

Collin didn't like the idea of going to the hospital, but he knew he wasn't going to talk Rebecca out of seeing her cousin. He needed to stop at his mom's house to get his weapons. He should have thought to put one in his car, but he hadn't been back there since the second attack on Rebecca and he wasn't keen on keeping them unsecured in the back of his car at a busy hospital. He would have to make getting over there a priority. Right after Rebecca saw her cousin.

He hated to believe this attack against Janice had anything to do with the girl holed up in the motel or the trafficking ring they'd uncovered. What would they do now and how could he protect everyone in her life? He would have to be on high alert while they were exposed at the hospital.

He felt her anger and worry flow off her as he drove to the hospital and parked in the garage, then led Rebecca inside to the fourth floor. She rushed to her cousin's bedside. Janice had taken quite a beating—her face was battered and her arm was in a cast.

"I can't believe this happened," Rebecca said as she gently hugged her cousin.

"What did happen?" Collin asked her. He had a sick feeling in the pit of his stomach that the ring had now involved Rebecca's family.

"I was returning home after my morning workout at the gym. I had just pulled into the garage when a man ducked under the doors and grabbed me. He demanded to know where you were, Rebecca. He was looking for you. When I told him I didn't know anything, he hit me." Tears flowed from her eyes. "I was so scared. I thought he was going to kill me."

Rebecca's face held fear as she stared up at Collin. She looked back at Janice. "Where was Matthew? Was he harmed?"

"No, he was with the nanny. They weren't at the house. I was alone. Rebecca, I was so afraid. I thought— I thought he was going to kill me."

Whoever was after Rebecca had just raised the stakes with this attack. If he would go after Rebecca's family to get to her that meant no one in her life was safe.

"I'll be right outside the door," he told Rebecca and she nodded.

He stepped outside and leaned against the wall. They had to find out who was behind these threats, and soon.

Rebecca was torn. She couldn't believe things had spiraled out of control so quickly. She had to protect Missy. She couldn't give up on her. But she also couldn't continue to put her family in danger. Her head was reeling at how her life had changed in just a couple of days.

She left her cousin to rest. As promised, Collin was leaning against the wall by Janice's door, his arms folded and his eyes alert. She felt better knowing he was there watching out for danger. She longed to step into his arms and have a good cry, but she couldn't put herself through that again. She couldn't allow herself to fall for Collin despite how she needed him now.

"How is she?" Collin asked her.

Rebecca thought about the bruises on her cousin's face and the cast on her arm. "She's frightened and confused. She's innocent in all of this. She didn't do anything wrong, yet she was still targeted." She looked at him. Sobs threatened to overtake her. "She's in danger because of me."

"You can't blame yourself for the actions of others. You weren't the one who attacked Janice or threatened Missy's life. She's in danger because of those people, not because of you."

"I'm afraid," she confessed. Terror surrounded her on all fronts but she was safe in Collin's arms.

"I promised you I would keep you safe, Rebecca, and I will."

His assurances were like a balm on an open wound. They felt so right and so wrong all at the same time. It made no sense for her to put her life, and now her family's lives, in his hands, but she knew she wouldn't survive this without him on her side.

God, is trusting him a mistake?

Where was He and why had He allowed another terrible thing to happen to someone she loved?

The elevator dinged and she saw the doors open. Her father stepped off carrying a vase of flowers and he frowned when he spotted her in Collin's embrace. She pulled away as he approached them.

"Dad, I'm glad you're here."

"Where have you been, Rebecca? I was worried when I couldn't reach you."

"I was with Collin." She didn't miss the disapproving look on her father's face, but she didn't care. He had no idea what she'd been through and she had no idea if he was involved. "There have been some more incidents and Collin has been there for me. I owe him my life, Dad."

Her father's eyes widened in shock at her statement, then his expression darkened. "What kinds of incidents? The kind that put your cousin the hospital?"

She felt herself redden. "It's my fault. The men who attacked Janice are targeting me."

He spun on Collin. "What have you gotten my daughter mixed up in?"

"It's not his fault," Rebecca insisted before Collin could even try to defend himself. "It's me they're after, Dad. They're trying to shut me up. All Collin has done is be there to protect me each time."

Her father grimaced. "What have you gotten yourself into, Rebecca? Why didn't you come to me?"

She didn't tell him it was because she wasn't certain he wasn't involved. "I think I've uncovered a human-trafficking ring operating in our area."

"Trafficking? What do you mean?"

"Yes, trafficking. Specifically, baby selling. These girls are being abducted and held until they give birth, then their children are stolen from them and they're put back into the process, being impregnated again to repeat the cycle."

"How can you know this? Does this have anything to do with that missing girl you've been searching for?"

"Yes, in a way. And now the ring wants to shut me up about it before I expose them for good."

Her father rubbed his face. She couldn't read his expression. Was that worry about his only child? Or worry that she was about to implicate him? She couldn't tell. "I don't like this one bit, Rebecca. It's too dangerous. Things like this need to be left to the police or the FBI."

Collin intervened. "I have a friend whose wife is an FBI agent. I'm waiting to hear back from her. Once I do, we'll take what Rebecca has uncovered to them."

Her father shook his head again. "You should have come to me with this. You know I have connections in the government. I'll make a few calls and see if we can't meet with someone tomorrow morning."

She started to protest. Would he make that call? And, if he did, could she trust the person he contacted? She hated suspecting her own father. It would make life so much simpler if she could trust him. She glanced at Collin, who nodded at her. It seemed he also wanted to believe that her father would never do anything to harm her, yet she couldn't forget Missy's words about seeing Mason Industries on the side of the building where she was being held.

"At the very least, you'll come home with me," her father said. "I can provide security for you."

She was about to protest when Collin spoke up.

"I think that's a good idea," he told Rebecca. "Your father's house has a built-in security system. It'll be safer for you there."

She didn't want to go home with her father. She wanted to stay with Collin at the hotel. She felt much safer with Collin, but how could she tell him that?

He touched her arm and leaned in to whisper close to her ear. "Don't worry. I'll be around. I won't leave you vulnerable, Rebecca."

She believed him. After the attack at her house, he'd promised not to leave her again.

Would he sleep outside the house in the rental car? She wouldn't allow that, not when her father's house had plenty of spare rooms. She turned back to her father. "I'll come home with you on one condition. Collin comes, too."

"What? You want him to stay at the house? No, Rebecca. No."

Her agitation rose. Surely he wasn't going to compromise on her security because of some petty grudge for something that happened over a decade ago. "You have plenty of guest rooms. He can stay in one of those. I know you have a security system, but I feel better having Collin around." He started to hesitate again and she grew frustrated. "Dad, let it go. What happened with me and Collin was a long time ago. We were just kids. We've both moved on and you should, too. Collin has been out of the country for years so he's the only person I know I can trust that isn't involved in this. Either he comes with us or I go with him."

Her father looked shocked. "What do you mean, he's the only one you can trust? You think I'm involved in this, Rebecca?"

"I have reason to believe there's a connection to Mason Industries." She folded her arms and stared him down, watching for any hint of concern. She hadn't meant to spring this accusation on him, but he seemed genuinely taken aback by her implication that he might be involved in human trafficking.

"I cannot believe you're saying this to me, Rebecca. You're my daughter. How can you believe I would ever hurt you? And Janice? You think I'm responsible for her getting attacked? She's like a daughter to me. I would never do anything to harm her. Or you." His indignation seemed real and she wanted to believe him. This was her father, after all. She wanted to trust him but she was scared.

Collin stepped between them. "Excuse me for saying so, Mr. Mason, but as you said earlier, you have connections. Some of those connections may not care as much about the safety of your daughter or your niece."

He squared his shoulders, insulted at Collin's suggestion, but he was right. Who knew the kind of men her father did business with? He took out his phone, ignoring Collin, and addressed Rebecca instead. "I'll call the housekeeper and have her make up your room—" he glared as he finished "—as well as one of the guest rooms. I'm going to go check on Janice and then call David to give him an update. He's beside himself with worry, since this happened while he was out of town. You know the alarm codes. I'll see you there later this evening."

He headed down the hall toward Janice's hospital room then disappeared inside.

"I've never seen him so hurt," she said, struck by how much it stung her to accuse her father of being involved. But how could she discount Missy's recollection of being in that warehouse or seeing the name on the side? "Thank you for agreeing to stay with us. I'll feel better knowing you're only a few doors down from me." She stared at him, wondering again if she was doing the right thing. "I'm putting a lot of faith in you, Collin. I'm trusting you with the lives and safety of my family. Everyone I care about."

"I know that, Rebecca, and I don't take that trust lightly. I know I've let you down in the past, but I'm not that same scared kid I once was. I've got the skills now to protect you and I promise I will do my best to keep you all safe."

Given his history of leaving her when she needed him most, she should worry about depending on him like she did, but she didn't because he was right. He'd gained the skills she needed now to keep her family safe, even if they were skills he'd obtained only because he'd abandoned her.

* * *

He was glad once they'd checked out of the hotel and moved into her father's house. The hotel had been a good option, but Rebecca's childhood home was gated with a top-of-the-line security system. He'd run afoul of the alarms and seen the gates slammed in his face many times as a kid. And Rebecca's father had always kept up with the latest in security. He imagined the upgraded system had all the bells and whistles. It would be a much better setup for keeping Rebecca safe. Plus, Collin had finally made the trip back to his mother's house to grab some clothes and his guns. He was prepared for anything.

He knew she wasn't thrilled with the idea of returning to her father's house, but she'd agreed to it because of Janice and Matthew, who were also staying there. She'd been reluctant to place her cousin in danger before, but danger had found her regardless and Collin knew Rebecca would rather be around to help keep her and Matthew safe. He thought of her confrontation with her father and was impressed with how she'd stood up to him. He'd waited years to witness something like that. She'd grown courageous and bold and it was a side that suited her. When they were younger, she'd done her own thing, but she'd always skirted around her father, avoiding any confrontations when she could. Today he'd seen the woman she'd become, and it was someone he'd always known she could be. He wished he'd been around to watch her grow into such a formidable woman.

But he'd also witnessed Bob Mason's reaction to her accusations. He'd seemed genuinely shocked and hurt by her words. If he was involved, Collin was convinced he wasn't the one in charge. If his company was being used in the crime of human trafficking, Collin tended to think he'd lost control of the situation when they targeted his only daughter.

He didn't miss the glare from Bob Mason as he headed for the stairs with his overnight bag.

"Rebecca told me about your mother. My condolences." His words were icy at best, and the way he looked at Collin told him nothing had changed about his opinion of Collin, but he appreciated that Bob made the effort.

"Thank you." No sense stirring up trouble for Rebecca, especially when her father had turned out to be right about him.

"How long are you staying?"

The underlying sentiment was clear—back off. It was true he'd made no plans to remain in town after closing up his mother's house, but neither Bob Mason's icy stare nor his money would convince him to leave Rebecca while she was still in danger. "I'll be here for as long as Rebecca needs me. I'd like to check your security systems if you don't mind."

"My house has ultramodern security features. Janice's husband, David, hired a great security firm to make sure everything was in order."

David again. Rebecca's father seemed to like this David Miller his niece had married. He must have everything Collin didn't—family money, a college education, a business background. All that Bob had hoped for Rebecca.

"I hear David works for you. Is that how he and Janice met?"

"Yes, I hired David right out of college and groomed him to take over the business. I had hoped Rebecca would want the company, but she's made it clear she has no interest in it."

"She seems content with her work."

"I've often wondered if she took a government job just to punish me for something. She's resented my wealth for years."

"That's not the Rebecca I remember."

"She's not the Rebecca you remember. It's been twelve years, Collin. She's grown more and more distant from me and the family during that time." Collin heard regret in his voice. He heaved out a long, weary sigh. "I thought once you were out of her life, I'd get my little girl back, but it didn't happen that way. You snatched her from her home and took her away."

"Excuse me, Mr. Mason, but her plans were always to be with me. We had to run off because of you and your resistance to Rebecca deciding what was best for her own life."

"She didn't know what was best for her own life," he insisted. "Otherwise, she would not have chosen you."

Collin grew angry. This was the same old argument all over again. "But she did choose me and you can't stand that, can you? She always wanted me."

He glared at Collin. "And look where it got her. Brokenhearted and abandoned in a dive apartment in New Orleans. You begged me to clean up your mess, as I recall, and I did, including writing you a check to disappear. Perhaps I should have been more specific. My ten thousand dollars was supposed to keep you out of town for good."

He cringed at the mention of that check. Yes, he'd taken money from Rebecca's father to pay off the hospital bills and it had hurt him to do so. But after failing to keep her and the baby safe, he'd had very little pride left and he hadn't wanted to leave Rebecca footing the bill for losing their child.

"I suppose life doesn't always turn out the way you thought it would. I'm sorry if you're distant from Rebecca, but that's because of you, not me. My only concern is keeping her safe."

"And how was it you showed up in town just in time to rescue her, Collin? That seems very convenient."

"Maybe it does." Or maybe it was God's will, after all. She'd been in danger for weeks before he'd arrived in town, but something had sent him out to the store on just the day Rebecca needed him most. He may be having a hard time seeing God working in his life lately, but he was thankful God had led him back to Moss Creek in time to help Rebecca.

"I suppose you're the one also filling her head with the idea that she can't trust her own father?"

"No, sir. In fact, I've been the one telling her you would never do anything that would hurt her. I know you love your daughter. That's never been your problem."

"Then why does she think I'm involved?"

"She has her reasons. I hope she's wrong

because she's already lost so much. I'd hate to see her lose you, too."

He hurried up the stairs to the room he'd be occupying and tossed his bag onto the bed. It was surreal that he was staying in the Masons' home. It felt wrong for him to be here, but he wasn't leaving as long as Rebecca was in trouble. He wouldn't abandon her again. Shame filled him for the way he'd run out on her all those years ago. She'd depended on him and he'd let her down. It was a guilt he hadn't been able to wash away no matter how many battles he fought or how many victories he won.

He'd let down the woman he loved.

But he was different now. How could he not be after all he'd seen and done. But one constant in his life hadn't changed. His feelings for Rebecca. He still cared about her even though he had no right to. He cared about what happened to her and it was more than simple friendship or a history of feelings from the past. He'd known it the moment he'd seen that man grab her outside the grocery store. She was important to him now.

But he wasn't the same man he'd been when he left her. He pulled out his gun and checked it. He'd grown into a man well suited to protect her and he would. Even if loving her was off the table.

"Are you settling in?"

He turned to find Rebecca standing in the doorway and his heart clenched. He put away his gun as the truth slammed against him like hitting a brick wall. Loving her would never be off the table for him.

"I hope you're not angry that I insisted you stay here," she said.

"No, Rebecca. I think it was a good idea. I'm glad you suggested it. We need to lay low, remain indoors until we find out who is after you or until we can get that meeting with the FBI."

She nodded. "I have a few vacation days I can take from work. I'll email my boss to let him know. But I have court on Wednesday that I can't miss and a meeting at the community center tonight."

He shook his head and turned back to unpacking his bag. "It's too dangerous for you to be out in public like that."

"I'm in charge of the night."

He sighed, not understanding why she would willingly put her life on the line to attend some meeting. "Can't you reschedule?"

"I run a program at the local community center for teens. It's called Life Skillz. I host workshops that teach teenagers—mostly foster kids, but everyone is welcome—about life skills like cooking, shopping, meal planning, money management. You know, things these kids need to know in order to succeed."

"It might not be safe for you." But even as he spoke, he knew his arguments were falling on deaf ears.

She persisted. "These kids have practically nothing. I can't let them down. I can't cancel on them, especially if all we're doing is hiding out. As long as Missy is hidden and safe, I have to think about the other kids under my care. They need me. Besides, if I cancel, that means they'll be out on the streets doing who knows what."

He was impressed. She wasn't fooling around when she said she wanted to help these kids. She was making a difference in their lives. It was such a contradiction to him. She'd grown up in privilege and wealth, yet she'd turned her back on it in order to reach out to those in need. She'd made it a mission in life. He admired her. That was the girl he remembered but it had only been a glimpse of the kindness inside of her when she was a girl. Now, she'd grown into a woman with convictions and values that changed lives.

But it didn't make his job of keeping her safe any easier.

"You haven't changed, have you? You're still stubborn and determined." He'd meant it as a compliment, but her expression clouded.

"Is that why you left me? Was I too difficult?"

His heart broke at her question and he jumped to respond. He didn't want her to have those doubts. "Absolutely not. I loved your determination. It was always one of your best qualities." He reached out and pushed a strand of hair from her face as she stared up at him, and he felt a piece of his heart rip away. How had he ever walked out on this woman? "It still is."

"But you didn't love it enough to stick around, did you?"

Her words—and the ache visible in her eyes—were enough to gut-punch him. It was time to address this. "My leaving back then was all about me, Rebecca. I was scared and overwhelmed. It had nothing to do with you."

"It felt like it had something to do with me. I was desperate and alone and you were just gone."

"I'm sorry."

She stared at him like she was expecting more. Some deep explanation that would explain away his foolish reaction to all that had happened. But there wasn't one. He'd been a scared kid in way over his head and he'd finally realized he couldn't handle the responsibilities.

Rebecca wiped away a tear that had slid down her cheek. "That's in the past. It doesn't matter anymore. What does matter are these kids and I won't let them down."

"Then I'm coming with you."

"Thank you, Collin. These kids need all the help they can get to survive."

And with a woman like Rebecca on their side, how could they lose?

Collin didn't like the risk Rebecca was taking, but he admired her determination to be there for the kids she mentored. He wished the place had private parking but it didn't, so he chose a spot across the street, as close as he could get to the door of the community center. He scanned the area before letting her get out. He didn't see evidence of anyone watching them or planning an attack. He opened the trunk and took out the box filled with sewing supplies, socks and patches, then walked with her inside. But he wasn't letting down his guard. She was exposed here and he didn't like it. This would be the perfect opportunity for someone to try to get to her when she was in public. He cringed at the large glass windows on the front of the building. He'd hoped at least to be in an area he could contain. Anyone could see in and that meant anyone could be out there watching and waiting for the opportunity to strike.

She unlocked the door and turned on the lights. "The first thing we have to do is set up. There are tables and chairs in the storage room. Tonight, I've got Melanie Donnelly coming in to teach the kids basic sewing skills, patches, darning socks, that sort of thing. She used to teach home economics at the high school until they cut the program two years ago. It's important that they know these skills."

He helped her line up the tables and chairs and set out the supplies, all the while keeping his eyes and ears open for any indication of trouble. "Where does the money come from?" he asked, noting that everything they needed seemed to be in the box.

"I set up a fund that operates on donations," she stated, but the way she averted her eyes told a different story. He wondered how many people were keen to donate to foster kids. Not many, he imagined, which made her sacrifices even greater. These kids were fortunate to have someone like Rebecca on their side.

Just before the top of the hour, kids started filing into the center. Collin was surprised by how many were there, especially on a Friday night. It was better that they were here than out on the streets, though. He watched Rebecca move through the crowd, speaking to each kid and offering her help. She wasn't just sitting on the sidelines. She was getting involved. He'd run away from his problems, but she'd stayed and jumped into life.

He liked this life she'd made for herself and found himself wishing he was a part of it. But what did he have to offer these kids? Sure, he had skills in weaponry and covert security. Certainly nothing he could share with kids. They surely saw enough gun violence on the streets and in video games. He knew kids, especially boys, needed male role models, but he couldn't even offer them tips on growing into a good man. You don't get to be called that when you'd done the things he'd done.

But Rebecca seemed to be flourishing just fine without him. Aside from crossing a baby-selling ring, she'd built a good life for herself and was making a difference. Was that why God had brought him here? To see how well she was doing without him? To give him peace about that terrible mistake he'd made? Or to punish him by making him witness that she didn't need him?

He shook his head and tried to get a grip. Was he really thinking about himself as part of her life? It was ridiculous. They'd had their time and he'd blown it. He had to stop thinking that way.

After the session, several of the kids stayed behind and helped put the chairs and tables back into the storage room, then cleaned up. Rebecca loaded what was left of the supplies back into the box and Collin carried them to the car as Rebecca shut off the lights and locked up.

He opened the trunk and placed the bins inside while Rebecca stopped to speak to a young girl who'd stayed behind. Collin waited and watched until she hugged the girl and hurried across the street. Once again, he was struck by her beauty and kindness. She was the most selfless person he'd ever known and he'd had her in his life and let her go. As she crossed the street, light from the streetlamp flowed over her, illuminating her beauty and the soft, delicate lines of her features.

His breath left him.

She was so beautiful.

Light hit her again and he turned to see a

car approaching. It was coming at her fast and seemed to be speeding up as it neared.

Another attack.

"Watch out!" Collin hollered as Rebecca crossed the street and the car gunned for her.

His instincts kicked in and he ran across the street, tackling Rebecca and knocking her out of the way just as the car swerved toward her. He rolled to his feet, grabbed his gun and fired at the car as it sped off. One shot hit the back window but the car didn't stop. It turned the corner and disappeared, its tires screeching against the asphalt.

Collin turned back to Rebecca on the ground. "Are you hurt?"

"I'm fine," she said.

His heart was pounding so loudly he nearly couldn't hear her response over his own pulse racing. Seeing her lying on the asphalt, old bruises mingling with new scrapes, caused anger to rip through him.

"What happened?" she asked. Her voice was strained and full of fear.

"That car just tried to run you down. Did you recognize the car or the driver?"

She shook her head. "I didn't even see it coming." She held his hand. "Collin, if you hadn't been here…"

"I knew coming here was a mistake."

"It was important."

"It nearly got you killed. Whoever is after you knows your routine. They knew they would find you here."

"I won't make apologies for caring for these kids," she said, jutting her chin stubbornly as he helped her to her feet. "And I won't give up on them. Any of them."

He did admire her determination, but how was he going to keep her safe when she insisted on putting herself in risky situations? He kicked himself for getting so wrapped up in Rebecca that he hadn't seen the danger coming. It had been a novice mistake. One that he wouldn't let happen again.

SIX

Her hands were shaking but it had nothing to do with the near miss she'd just experienced and everything to do with Collin. Being so close to him again was beginning to wear on her nerves. She was trying to remain cold and aloof but it was hard. This was the man she'd loved enough to marry and have a child with.

It seemed like a lifetime ago that they'd been so happy. And it was a lifetime. She wasn't that girl any longer. She was a mature woman with a life of her own. But she'd never forgotten how it felt to be in love. She'd counted on him to be there for her, but he'd let her down. Now, so much was at stake.

Ignoring her feelings wasn't working and neither was denying them. She was falling for him again and she couldn't allow that to happen. She had to put the brakes on this once and for all. Collin was being kind, possibly even trying to make up for the way he'd left her all those years ago, but she didn't want his pity or his guilty conscience. She had to think about Missy and keeping the girl safe.

Two sheriff's office cruisers arrived and the area was soon surrounded. Kent got out of his car and approached them, his face hard and angry. "I suppose now you're going to tell me I had a hand in this, too?" He stared from one to the other. "I want to know what is going on and I want the truth." He looked at Rebecca. "Why does someone want you dead? And don't try to act like you don't know. I think it's time you come clean with me about what exactly is going on here. I can't protect you if you continue to keep me in the dark."

Was Collin right? Had she been a target tonight because someone knew her routine? Everyone in her life knew about the foundation and her work with Life Skillz, and she'd done quite a bit of publicity trying to raise donations. She glanced at Collin. He was trying so hard to protect her, but maybe it was too much for him to handle alone.

She glanced at Collin. "What do you think?"

He sighed and rubbed his face. "We need him, Rebecca."

Her hands were shaking with fear but she

had no choice but to trust him. "The girl who went missing, Missy Donovan."

"What about her?"

"She's not missing anymore. She showed up at my door a few nights ago. She escaped from her abductors. They'd been holding her captive until she gave birth. They took her baby from her, Kent, and sold it. And she's not the only one. She was only one of many girls being held there."

His face paled and he stumbled over his next words. "What? She was kidnapped and she escaped? Where is she now?"

She hesitated. Missy had been safe at the motel so far and she didn't want to jeopardize that.

When he noticed her hesitancy, he continued. "We need to get her into protective custody and I need to question her."

"She won't," Rebecca said. "She's too frightened of police. She says she saw someone with a badge talking with her captors."

"Can't you tell her there's nothing to be afraid of?"

Rebecca only stared at him and Kent got the point that she wasn't so sure there wasn't anything to be frightened of.

He locked eyes with her. "It wasn't me, Rebecca. If there's a dirty cop involved in this, it's even more important to find out who it is. They'll find her eventually and she'll be killed or reabducted."

She shook her head. "I'm sorry. I can't." She couldn't risk anyone else knowing Missy's location. She didn't know if she was doing the right thing or not, but telling him felt wrong.

Kent heaved a sigh of exasperation. "I can't believe you don't trust me."

She stared at him but didn't flinch. "I'm not sure anymore who I can trust."

She turned to Collin as Kent walked off and he put his arm around her and pulled her into a hug. "It's going to be okay. We're going to get through this."

"I don't like this feeling," she told him. "I've spent my life trusting people and now everyone I know is suspect." She glanced up at him. "Everyone except you." She touched his arm, sending sparks through her skin. "I'm so thankful you're here with me, Collin. You're the only person I know I can trust."

She saw a flash of something in his face. Was that regret that he'd gotten so involved in this? It was such a messed up situation.

She turned and saw Kent on his phone, but he was watching her. Was she doing the right thing by not trusting him? Or was she putting Missy's life in even more danger?

Rebecca gathered the papers she'd printed out. After being nearly run down on the street, the rest of the evening had been quiet. She didn't like being cooped up in this house and always looking over her shoulder for danger. She was ready to go back to her ordinary, simple life.

She glanced at Collin in the next room. He was busy, too. She had to admit, she would be sad to see him leave once this was all over. If there was a bright side to this situation, it was seeing him again. She pulled at the chain around her neck and fingered the ring on it. She hadn't worn this ring since returning home after he left, but she'd never been able to fully put it away. Janice had once questioned her about it, but Rebecca had insisted she'd found it and liked it, pretending it held no significance to her at all. That had been hard, but thankfully, Janice hadn't pressed the matter. These days, Rebecca mostly wore it beneath her shirt to avoid the questions.

She pulled herself away from watching Collin and the little-girl feelings his presence brought up and tried to concentrate on the work she'd had sent over from her office.

She had other kids that needed her besides just Missy and the teens from Life Skillz. She had several cases to prepare for court. If she dropped the ball on any one of them, a child could fall through the cracks in the system and wind up in a bad situation.

On court day, they saw at least forty cases and Rebecca had to be prepared to make recommendations for each one. It was her job to evaluate a child's living situation and act in the best interest of the child. In Missy's case, her drug-addicted mother had tried to regain custody of her several times but had failed the court-mandated drug tests. She'd finally given up her rights and turned the girl over to the system. But other kids had different stories. Some parents fought hard to get their kids back and she admired those who changed their lives and did what they needed to do for their child. But then there were the parents who saw nothing wrong with their living situations and believed their child, or children, had been taken from them unjustly.

She glanced at one file that illustrated the latter. A ten-year-old girl named Olivia had been removed from a home because of abuse by her mother's boyfriend. Olivia's mother was trying to get her daughter back but refused to cut ties with her abusive partner. Rebecca didn't enjoy taking away someone's kids, but she understood the need to give a child a safe environment in which to grow up. Olivia's mother had chosen to put the attention of a man before the safety of her child. She didn't know if she was abused herself, although Rebecca suspected it. But it wasn't her place to make that call. Her job was to decide what was in the best interest of the child and, in this case, it was permanent removal. When they went back to court she would make her recommendation to the judge.

She glanced up and saw Collin standing in the doorway watching her. He looked like he had something important to say. "What's up?"

"I've been thinking about this issue with Kent. You've been giving him information piece by piece. It's not working. We need to tell him where Missy is."

"Collin, I don't think—"

"We need to trust him with this at least until we can get in touch with the FBI." Before she could protest again, he continued with his thoughts. "It's been several days already since Missy escaped. The bruises on her are starting to fade and any information she has about the ring's location may be time sensitive, as well. If they can't find her, they may pick up and change locations. If that happens, we will never find out who is behind this ring, who is trying to hurt you or if they'll ever stop."

She saw the fear in his eyes at the idea that he might not be able to end this.

"I know she's afraid, but we need to bring her in to be questioned. We can't wait much longer."

She knew he was right. Days had passed and Missy hadn't budged on the topic of talking to the police. Rebecca had thought she was doing the right thing by trying to keep Missy safe on her own, but the threat was getting too high to keep this secret any longer.

She nodded and pushed away her work. "Okay. Let's go over there now and talk to her."

He looked surprised that she'd agreed with him but didn't question her change of heart. They got into Collin's car and headed across town.

Rebecca was afraid pushing the girl would make her close up, but hiding out at the motel wasn't a long-term solution for Missy's protection, or for Rebecca's. They needed to discover who was behind this ring and bring them down, and they needed what Missy knew to do it.

Her cell phone rang and Rebecca saw the number of the motel on her screen. She answered it, her heart jumping as Missy's panicked voice cried out to her.

"They're here, Rebecca! They're here!"

"Who is it?" she asked, trying to remain cool while calming down the girl so she could find out what was happening.

Collin must have heard the panic in her voice because his face registered shock as he listened to her.

"Missy, talk to me. Tell me what's happening."

"The van. I saw the van pull into the parking lot. They're coming for me."

She spotted Collin on his phone and heard him mention Kent's name. He was calling to tell him about Missy. Bless this man for knowing just what she needed him to do. She couldn't get off the phone with Missy to call the police.

She heard the fear in Missy's voice as she whispered, "They're here. They're at the door."

Rebecca thought she heard someone in the background urging Missy on as she and Collin hopped into the car and headed that way. It sounded like a male voice, but she couldn't make out the words.

"Lock yourself in the bathroom," Rebecca told her. "We're on our way and so are the police."

A loud banging noise came over the phone and Missy screamed at the top of her lungs. It sounded like she dropped the phone, then Rebecca heard her cries for help. "No! Stop! Don't! Leave me alone!"

Rebecca turned to Collin. They were trying to bust down the door. Missy was being abducted again and they could do nothing to stop it. She'd never felt so helpless before.

"Hold on," Collin said, gripping the steering wheel even tighter and speeding up.

All Rebecca could do was listen to the screams of a frightened girl on the other end of the line and pray that they reached her in time.

The call from Missy had Rebecca rattled and with good reason. If someone had tracked down Missy, she was in real trouble. Collin had phoned Kent and relayed the news about the phone call they'd just received and given him the location of the motel. All worries about not involving the police had to be put aside now.

He drove like a madman across town and was glad they had been on their way, but he was still surprised to see a white van parked in front of Missy's door and a large man dragging her kicking and screaming from the room. Collin recognized him as the same man who had attacked Rebecca the night they'd first reunited.

He screeched the car to a halt and grabbed his weapon. "Stay inside," he ordered Rebecca as he slammed the car door and called out to the men. "Put the girl down," he shouted, raising his gun as he moved toward them.

Another man jumped from the van and shot at them. Collin jerked behind the door as he fired back at them. He heard Rebecca scream from inside. "Get down," he told her.

He didn't want to shoot at the van again because Missy might get hurt, but he knew if these men got away with her, she might be dead regardless. He returned fire, praying she wouldn't be harmed by his bullets. As one man fired, the other dragged her into the waiting van and hopped inside. The other man jumped into the van's passenger seat as the first drove. The van roared away and Collin chased after them, shooting. Behind him, he heard Rebecca screaming. He spun around. She was about to run past him and chase after the van, but he grabbed her and scooped her up into his arms to prevent her from running after them. It was too late. There was nothing either of them could do.

Rebecca fell to the ground sobbing and all he could do was put his arms around her and hold her.

The police sirens announced Kent was on his way. He pulled out his phone.

"We're nearly there," Kent said when he answered.

"Missy is gone. Two men in a white van took her. The license plate was obscured. No logo info on the van but they were headed north on Lexington Avenue. One of the men who grabbed her was the same man who attacked Rebecca at the grocery store."

"We're here."

Several cruisers rolled into the parking lot and screeched to a stop. Five deputies poured out. Kent hurried toward them.

"I've got a BOLO out on the van. I also sent a car heading that way to search for it. Tell me what happened."

"Like I told you on the phone, Rebecca got a call from Missy. She said someone was trying to get into the room. She recognized the men as part of the baby-selling ring."

They walked over to Rebecca and Kent glared down at her. "This is your fault," he told her. "I could have protected her if you had just trusted me." He stormed off and Rebecca put her hands over her face.

"I promised her she would be safe. I promised I would keep her safe."

"We'll find her," Collin said, squatting beside her. "We won't stop until we find her."

He knew what it was like to let someone down and he hated to think Rebecca would ever have to feel that kind of guilt. He made himself a promise that that wouldn't happen.

Rebecca and Collin stayed at the motel well into the night as Kent and his team pored over the scene. It looked like Missy had tried locking herself in the bathroom as Rebecca had suggested because the attackers had busted down two doors, the front entrance and the bathroom, to get to her.

Finally, Collin drove them back to the mansion. Rebecca stretched out on the sofa instead of heading upstairs to her room. The sun was already dawning on a new day, a day where Missy was once again a prisoner. She knew she wouldn't be able to sleep and she had no more tears, no more anger or bitterness to spew at Kent or anyone. She was spent.

Collin brought her a glass of water and sat

beside her. He looked like he was about to apologize to her again, but she didn't want to hear it.

Instead of apologizing, he held her hand and made her a promise. "I won't stop until we bring these people down."

Despite the fact that they still had no more information about the ring than before, his assurances made her feel better. Missy was not alone in this...and neither was she. One question still ran through her mind. How had they found Missy?

Her father walked into the room carrying an accordion folder. "May I speak with you, Rebecca?"

She sighed. She was too worn out to listen to another of his angry lectures about Collin. Couldn't he look at them and tell they'd been up all night? "What is it, Dad?"

"In the spirit of being transparent, I have something for you." He held out the folder to her. "As you know, Mason Industries owns many commercial properties, including some that are no longer in use. I asked my secretary to make a list. I've also asked her to list the current statuses of each property and if they're being rented out and to whom."

Rebecca sat up and took the folder. She flipped through the papers then looked up at her father. He'd just handed them another avenue to finding Missy. She was unable to come up with words powerful enough to express her gratitude besides a simple thank-you.

"If one of my properties is being used to intentionally cause harm, I want to know it."

"This means a lot to me."

"I hope it helps."

It did help. He looked so anxious to win her over. That he'd taken this step made her believe him when he said he wasn't involved. She stood and hugged him, something she hadn't done in a long while, and he hugged her back and smiled.

"Well, good night."

"Good night, sir," Collin said.

Rebecca pulled out the papers and started looking through them and Collin took the spot beside her.

"What should we do with these?" she asked him. "Should we check out every building?"

"Missy couldn't have come very far. I say we start with the ones in a hundred-mile radius and work our way out from there. That's a lot of driving and I don't like you being out in the open so much."

His brow crinkled and she thought he was about to say they couldn't go. Or worse, that he would take care of it alone. She had to follow up on this lead.

"I know it's a risk, but I think we have to try."

"And if you were right and your father is involved—"

"If he is then the place we're looking for probably won't even be in this stack." She stopped and looked at him. "But I believe him, Collin. Or at least, I believe he's trying to help us." She realized how long it had been since she'd believed in anything or anyone. She'd spent so many years hiding, protecting herself from pain, that she was struggling to even trust her own father. But she wanted to and it felt right.

"I believe him, too," Collin told her and she breathed a sigh of relief. She'd grown out of practice with her trust muscle so she was glad to have the second opinion of someone she seemed to have no trouble in trusting. That should worry her, but it didn't. She'd fallen into accepting Collin's help as simply as she'd fallen in love with him all those years ago. He made it easy to engender trust. One of his strengths had always been that his charm and easy smile made him likable, but his conviction and integrity had made him truly trustworthy.

Until that night when his integrity had failed and he'd abandoned her.

She hated the way her devious heart kept tossing that back in her face. He'd apologized for his actions multiple times. Didn't people sometimes deserve second chances? Didn't she deserve a second chance at happiness?

"Looks like we'll be doing some driving today," he said as he mapped out twelve commercial buildings within a hundred-mile radius of the city." He stopped and looked at her. "We're only doing reconnaissance, Rebecca. If we do find something suspicious, we can't rush in alone. Promise me, we'll call Kent or the local PD if we find what we're looking for."

"I promise," she told him. It felt good to not be alone in this any longer.

Despite having no sleep the previous night, they spent the day driving and located all twelve buildings. Four sat empty, while the rest were occupied with what seemed like normal business operations. Missy hadn't said anything about other people being around. In fact, she'd made it seem like the place she'd been held was abandoned. Rebecca marked each off her list one by one as they drove.

They found the last building on the list two

hours outside of Moss Creek. "It's close to the highway," Rebecca noted, feeling optimistic for the first time all day.

The old warehouse was set back off the road and trees and bushes had grown wild around it. The parking lot was empty so Collin pulled close to the building. As Rebecca got out of the car, she noticed the words Mason Industries printed across the side of the building facing the highway. Several of the other abandoned factories had had the name printed on the side, but with the inclusion of the highway, this had to be the spot where Missy had been held.

She hurried toward the front of the building with Collin at her heels. She heard no noises from inside, and when she looked through a window, the building seemed empty.

"Rebecca, look."

She turned to find Collin crouched near two long black lines. "Skid marks, and they haven't faded so they must be recent." He stood and pulled his gun from its holster. "Let me go inside first."

Collin tried the door and found it unlocked.

"It's probably nothing," he told her, trying not to get her hopes up, but she had a feeling in her gut that this was the place.

He scanned the area for anyone hiding. She

followed and let him take the lead. She wasn't looking to get killed and respected Collin's ability to keep her safe.

He finally put his gun back into its holster. "The place is empty."

She glanced around. The warehouse showed no evidence of anyone being around, but it was missing one thing an empty building would have collected—dust. Where were the spiderwebs in the corners or the dust on the floor? Someone had been here recently and cleaned. They must have cleared out after Missy had escaped as Collin had feared, but Rebecca was convinced someone had been here.

"What do you think?" Collin asked her.

"I think this is the place they were holding her."

He moved toward a door on the opposite side of the building and opened it. It led down a flight of steep stairs to an underground storage room. Again, Rebecca noticed the lack of dust and spiderwebs.

She glanced at a spot on the floor and called Collin over. "I think it's blood."

He straightened. "We should call Kent. He can arrange to have this place given a good forensic sweep."

She nodded her agreement. They would

find nothing else here that would lead them to where the kidnappers were going.

They walked back to the car, but once she had buckled up, she stared at the building and felt Missy slipping away. They'd found the place she'd been held only to be too late to help her. "We missed her," Rebecca said. "If they moved their operation, they could be anywhere by now."

Collin reached for her hand and she curled it around his, loving the warmth of his eyes and the strength of his hand. "We'll find her," he assured her. "We found this place, didn't we? We won't give up."

She was thankful he was with her on this journey and he was a constant stream of support for her. But she was also aware how dependent she was becoming upon him and that frightened her. Collin had broken her heart years ago. Was she really ready to risk it on him again?

The warehouse was in the neighboring county but Kent was able to get permission from that sheriff's office to bring in his own people to give the abandoned building a thorough once-over. He told Collin and Rebecca the local sheriff wasn't interested in pouring his resources into an abandoned property.

"Maybe if they'd cared enough, they might have noticed girls being held hostage right under their noses." Rebecca's tone was unforgiving and rightly so, Collin thought, but this ring was apparently operating under everyone's noses. If she hadn't pressed to find Missy, who knew how long it might have gone unnoticed. She was the real hero here.

Collin waited while Kent and his team finished their sweep. He finally approached them. "We did find traces of blood inside, but it's not substantial. It looks like the place has been cleaned. They were covering their tracks. We were able to talk with people along the route here that saw vans like the one you described at the motel coming and going from here constantly."

Collin sighed. So this place had been used for trafficking women. He stared at the big, painted letters on the side of the building that read Mason Industries and knew this was where a young girl had been kept. Terrible things had been done to her here and no one had been the wiser. She'd been invisible, another foster care kid who might have slipped through the cracks if not for Rebecca.

"So what do we do now?" he asked Kent.

"I've still got a BOLO out on the van and

we're still processing evidence from the scene at the motel."

Collin's phone rang and he glanced at the screen. The number that appeared wasn't familiar to him but he answered it, anyway, and he was glad he did. It was the FBI agent he'd left a message for two days ago.

"I'm glad you called," Collin told her and she listened while he explained what was happening. When he was done, he handed the phone to Kent, who also answered questions then put her on speaker.

"We're wrapping up a sting operation now," she told both men once she'd gathered all the facts. "Once we're done here, I'll head that way and I'll have someone in the office gathering intel in the meantime. You can expect me and my team in the next few days."

Collin thanked her then ended the call. Rebecca would be glad to know the FBI was also getting involved in the case as they'd originally planned. But that was before Missy had been found and taken again. His hope was that they would find her alive once this was all said and done, but at the very least he would settle for the justice of taking down the ring once and for all.

He walked to Rebecca and shared the good news with her. She gave him a smile, but the dark circles around her eyes told him this ordeal was taking its toll on her. She needed to rest and recuperate, but he knew she wouldn't be able to truly rest until she knew what had happened to Missy. Perhaps once the FBI was here, she would find the rest she needed.

"There's nothing more we can do here," he told her. "Kent will call us when he finds something." He saw the despondency on her face and felt the need to reassure her. "We will find her," he promised.

He saw a moment's hesitation in her eyes. He'd let her down before but that wasn't going to happen again. He held her hand. "I'm here for you, Rebecca, and I'm not going anywhere. I won't let them hurt you. We'll figure out who is behind this."

"I hope you're right." She leaned into him and he soaked in her presence before recalling how a moment's weakness, a moment of taking her in, had distracted him and nearly cost her life when that car had tried to run her over yesterday. Her welfare had become so important to him in only a few short days. He couldn't allow his judgment to be clouded that way again.

He broke off their embrace and ushered her to the car. When she glanced up at him in curiosity, he put on his game face. He had to treat this like any other dangerous situation he'd been a part of. He had to set up boundaries and protect the inside.

Only this time he was guarding two things—Rebecca's life...and his heart.

SEVEN

His phone rang even before they made it back to Rebecca's father's house. Collin checked the ID. "It's Kent." He pressed the button to answer the call and put it on speaker mode. "That was quick. Did you find something?" He saw Rebecca's eyes widen in excitement at the prospect of a break in the case.

"Not at the warehouse, but I just got word about some fingerprints we lifted from the motel."

"Whose are they?" Rebecca asked.

"They belong to a seventeen-year-old kid named Dylan Kepler."

"That was Missy's boyfriend," Rebecca said. "Why were his prints at the motel? Do you think he's involved?"

"I don't know. We found a lot of partial prints. It is a motel, after all. But his prints were all over the door and in the bathroom including the window. It looks like he might have climbed out the bathroom window."

Rebecca covered her mouth as she recalled something. "I thought I heard someone else in the room with Missy when she was taken. It sounded like someone was urging her to leave. It had to have been Dylan."

"But how did he know she was there?"

"Maybe she called him, hoping to see a familiar face. Someone to comfort her." He hated to think she'd reached out to the boy only to have him turn her over to the ring. "Is there any chance he's involved in human trafficking?" Collin asked.

Kent sighed. "His record isn't spotless, but it's mostly parking tickets and a couple of misdemeanor shoplifting arrests. That's how we have his prints on file. Nothing that indicates any violent disposition."

Collin turned to Rebecca. "Did you speak to him after Missy vanished? What was your take on him?"

"I did. He seemed like a good kid to me. He got good grades and was preparing for college. And he seemed to care about Missy."

"We should question him again."

"I've got my hands full here," Kent said. "I could send one of my guys over there but—"

"We'll go," Rebecca interjected. "We'll talk to him."

Kent sighed. "That's what I figured. Let me know if I need to intervene."

Collin ended the call then headed for a park where Rebecca told him teens in the area sometimes congregated in the evenings.

He parked the car and they got out. Several people yelled greetings to Rebecca and she responded accordingly. Again, he was struck by the connection she was making with these teens.

"There he is," she said, pointing toward a scrawny, dark-haired kid on the other side of the basketball court. He wasn't playing ball but was hanging out with two other boys.

As they approached, Dylan turned, saw them and took off running.

Collin chased after him, catching him as he attempted to climb over a fence. His small frame made Collin think he wasn't the athletic type, and it was a good thing. If the teen had made it over the fence, he could have been gone.

"Why did you run, Dylan?" Collin demanded and only then did Collin notice the black eye and scrapes on his knuckles. This kid had recently taken a beating and done his best to beat back.

Rebecca caught up with them, her own bruises shining in the light from the streetlamp. "What happened to you, Dylan?"

"It was nothing. Just a fight. I already told you I don't know where Missy is," he said.

"And you don't seem to care. Now, tell us who did this to you."

Dylan turned to look at him. "Who are you?"

"A friend helping Rebecca find Missy. We need you to answer a few questions."

"Look, I told you when Missy first went missing I didn't know what happened to her. That hasn't changed."

"Then I'll ask different questions. When was the last time you saw Missy?"

"I told you. I saw her the night before she left. She told me she wanted space to figure things out."

"What kinds of things?"

"She didn't think she wanted to keep the baby."

Rebecca gasped. "That's not true. She was looking forward to having it."

"She changed her mind. She knew having a kid at sixteen would be hard on both of us."

"She was too far along to end the pregnancy, Dylan."

"Look, she wasn't the only one with plans.

I'm going to college. I got a full academic scholarship to the University of Mississippi. A baby just would have—" he sighed "—it would have ruined everything."

"You're sounding more and more like a guilty man, Dylan." Collin took his arm and forced him to sit on a bench. "Listen to me, Dylan. A girl is dead, probably murdered. She was abducted and her baby stolen from her before she was found dead from an overdose. If the same thing happens to Missy, guess who's going to pay for that? You are. You'll go down for kidnapping and murder."

"I didn't have anything to do with that."

"But you knew she escaped her abductors and was back in town, didn't you? You were in her motel room. Did you call those goons and tell them where she was?"

"No, I wouldn't do that." He pulled a hand through his hair. "Look, I knew she was back. She called me. I went over there to see her. I guess they were following me."

"Who was following you?"

"I don't know who they were. It was two big guys. They busted in the door. We tried to go out through the bathroom window. I thought she was right behind me but when I turned around, one of them grabbed her. I tried to help her but this guy threw me against the wall. When I woke up, she was gone and the police were there. I took off. I care about Missy. I didn't want anything bad to happen to her."

"Tell us what you do know about the day she disappeared."

"I told Missy I didn't want the baby and she freaked. She wasn't going to have an abortion so I thought I had convinced her to give up the baby for adoption. We talked about it and she said she'd think about it. There's this guy that my friend Rodney heard about. He said he'll pay good money for a baby. If you go through the adoption agencies, they don't give you anything. So I set up a meeting with him."

Rebecca frowned. "That doesn't sound like anything Missy would be involved in."

"She didn't like it but I convinced her to go with me just to listen to what the guy said. I think she went only to shut me up about it. She probably thought she'd listen to what the man said then have months to think about it."

"What happened?" Collin asked.

"We met this guy behind the old shopping mall. He said he was one of those baby doctors and he wanted to check Missy out. I helped her climb into the van so he could listen to her heartbeat. The next thing I knew, they were tossing me out the back and telling me if I mentioned anything about them, they'd kill me. I asked them about the money and the guy gave me five hundred bucks."

Collin saw the horror written across Rebecca's face as she addressed him. "You should have gone to the police. Or at the very least told me that when I asked you about her."

"I was scared. They threatened to kill me if I said anything."

"And what did you think they were going to do to Missy?"

"He said they were only going to keep her until the baby was born then she could come back home."

"Who was this man, Dylan? Did he give you his name?"

"He only called himself Jack, but his real name is Dr. Jack Rayburn. He has a practice in Jackson."

"How do you know that?"

"One of my foster sisters is pregnant and she had to go see him because she's a high-risk pregnancy. She brought home the pamphlet of information they give you on the first visit. I saw his photo on it and recognized him. I thought about calling him, demanding to know where Missy was." Color tinged his face. "I guess I was too much of a coward."

Collin rubbed his face. He wanted to let this kid have it, but he couldn't. He saw himself in him too much to stay really angry at him. He was just a scared kid who'd gotten in over his head. One dumb idea and his life was ruined. He pulled at his arm, forcing him to stand. "Let's go, Dylan."

"Where are you taking me?"

"To the police station. You're going to tell them exactly what happened and you'd better pray they find her alive or you'll go down for accessory to murder."

Dylan hung his head, but he didn't protest as they walked to the car. He got inside and remained quiet until they reached the sheriff's office, where, true to his word, he recounted to Kent when he returned from the warehouse scene just what he'd told them about the mysterious Dr. Rayburn, who'd snatched his girlfriend right off the street.

Kent led Dylan into an interview room and listened to what the boy had to say. Once he was done, Kent stepped out and shook his head. "I should have listened to you from the start," he told Rebecca.

She cut him no slack. "Yes, you should have."

"What are you going to do now, Kent?"

"I'm not letting him out of my sight until

the FBI arrives. He has an outstanding warrant on some unpaid parking tickets. It's only misdemeanor charges but it'll allow me to hold him for a couple of days, at least until the FBI gets here. I know they'll want to question him about this mysterious doctor. He's at least a witness, if not an accomplice to an abduction, and I don't want him running off before then."

Collin glanced at Rebecca as she watched Dylan through the window into the interview room. "What do you think?" he asked her. "Is he involved?" He had his own theory on the boy's guilt or innocence, but he was curious what she thought.

She sighed. "I don't think he's involved in the ring, but he bears some responsibility for Missy being taken. But this Dr. Rayburn should be our main concern. We need to speak to him."

"Absolutely not," Kent said. "We'll let the FBI take on the doctor."

"That's not good enough," Rebecca insisted. "Missy can't wait for the FBI to arrive."

She walked off, leaving Kent to shake his head. "She's not going to wait for the FBI, is she?"

"Nope." He had a strong feeling they would

be driving to Jackson next. It was Sunday night so they would have to wait until the offices opened tomorrow morning. At least they'd be able to get a night's sleep. "I'll let you know what happens."

He shook Kent's hand then caught up to Rebecca as she got into the car.

A pained expression settled on her face as she buckled up. "I can't believe Dylan knew all this time and didn't tell anyone," she said. "How could he do that?"

"He's a scared kid. He didn't know what to do."

"Missy is probably scared, too, but he didn't think about that. He was only thinking of himself and how having a baby would affect his life. He didn't care about hers."

Collin leaned against the steering wheel. He could relate to the boy on that level so much. "I know that fear, remember?"

"As far as I recall, you didn't sell me to a baby-trafficking ring to get rid of your problem."

No, he'd wanted that child. Something to link him to Rebecca forever. Unfortunately, God had had other plans for them. Now it was his failure that linked them. He understood her pain, but he also knew what it was like to be a kid and told a baby was coming. He couldn't condone Dylan's tactics or his failure to tell someone, but he understood what the boy was feeling.

"Do you remember the night you told me you were pregnant? I felt my whole world crumbling around me. You were looking at me like you wanted me to be happy about the baby, but all I could think about was my future blowing away like the wind. It's a big load for such a young guy."

"You didn't have to bear it alone, Collin. I was in it, too. I think I wanted to hear you say you were happy and everything was going to be okay so I wouldn't be so scared."

He looked at her, surprised to hear that. She hadn't shown him the least bit of reservation when she'd told him she was pregnant. "You were scared? You never showed it."

"A baby wasn't really in my plans, either, at least not so soon." She reached for his hand and held it, locking eyes with him. "But you were in my plans, Collin. When I looked at my future, it always included you."

He swallowed hard, fighting back a rush of emotions that threatened to send him to his knees if he hadn't already been sitting. The love he'd felt for her had been true and real and it had never faded. "Me, too," he whispered, pressing his hand against hers.

But her eyes changed. They grew colder and she pulled her hand away. "Then you left me. I depended on you and you abandoned me."

Her abrupt tone stung but it didn't alter the truth about him. "I can't change what happened," he told her. "I can only say I'm not the same person I was back then, Rebecca. I was a kid, young and scared. I know I let you down long before I ever left. If I had been a better provider, maybe you wouldn't have lost the baby."

She turned to him and he saw pain and regret flashing in her brown eyes. "That wasn't your fault."

Yet he'd taken the blame from day one. "I should have been able to afford a better doctor. Or if I'd taken you back to your father's house, he could have gotten you the care you needed."

"I wasn't lacking in medical care, Collin. It just happened. There's no rhyme or reason to it. Only God knows the purpose."

"How can there be a purpose for losing a child? It was a punishment."

"No, it wasn't."

"Yes, it was. It was a punishment for me thinking I could ever have you, ever give you the kind of life you deserved to have." He still beat himself up over how high the price for his failures had been. "You got caught up in the wake of my punishment, which makes it all the worse. You always ended up paying the price for my decisions. I couldn't allow that to happen any longer. You deserved better, Rebecca. That's why I left."

Anger flashed through her. "Who were you to make that decision for me? You. My father. You both wanted to tell me what was best for me, but I knew what was best for me, Collin. It was you. All I ever wanted was you. I didn't care about the money or the lack of it. I wanted to be with you and I wanted to have babies with you and when we lost the first one, the only thing that got me through it in those early days was knowing that one day when we were both ready we could have another and another and another. I wasn't going to give up until I was holding your child in my arms." Tears slipped down her face. "When you left, you broke more than my heart, Collin. You shattered those dreams."

He was stunned by her outburst, but she wasn't wrong. He had made the decision to leave without consulting her, without even telling her. He'd just run, and that's not what adults were supposed to do.

He made up his mind right then. He couldn't

change what had happened between him and Rebecca and he would never have a future with her, but he had finally found something he had to give to kids like Dylan. He could teach them to stay and face their fears like a man should do.

The next morning, Rebecca was online looking up everything she could find on Dr. Jack Rayburn as Collin made the sixty-mile drive to the city of Jackson. Rayburn had a clinic there where he saw high-risk pregnancies.

"That would certainly make sense with a baby-selling ring," Collin said when she told him. "They would need a good physician to make sure the women were healthy or else they couldn't sell the babies."

But how involved was Rayburn in the ring? Was he just the help or the guy behind it? Rebecca thought of Missy and wished they could ask her about Rayburn. Would she have been able to identify him as the doctor who'd worked on her? Did he know where she was right now?

Collin could obviously see what she was thinking. "We're only here to question this man, Rebecca. We have no proof he was involved in anything and we're taking the word of a teenage boy who, by his own admission, allowed his pregnant girlfriend to be abducted. He could have been lying to us."

She knew he didn't believe that. He'd instantly bonded with Dylan over their shared history. The thing was, she believed him, too. "I know he could be lying, but he gave us this doctor's name and he does exist. He's also an obstetrician."

She had a feeling about this doctor. They were finally catching a break and she hoped he would lead them to Missy and the rest of the girls he'd helped kidnap.

"If he's involved, he's certainly not going to admit knowing Missy, but it'll give us an opportunity to gauge his reaction. We can't go in there confrontational or he won't see us. We'll need a cover story just to get through the door."

He was right. She hadn't considered that angle. "What should we say?"

"We'll tell the receptionist we're a married couple—"

"Which we are."

He shot her a surprised glance. They hadn't spoken much of the fact that they were legally still married.

He continued. "We're thinking of starting a family and are interviewing obstetricians."

A lump formed in her throat. That cover story was too close to the truth for her comfort. Given her history of losing a child, it wouldn't be a stretch to be looking for a high-risk doctor, either. The pain that memory brought should have faded years ago, but it was still strong and raw, and being with Collin only seemed to bring it to the surface.

She'd never truly gotten over it. How could she when her entire life had been falling apart? She'd not only lost a child, but she'd also been abandoned by her husband. And she'd kept it all a secret from everyone she knew. It was no wonder she hadn't been able to get over it. She hadn't even dealt with it, had just hidden it away in a corner of her heart and nursed her pain in the intervening years.

He reached across the seat and gave her hand a squeeze as if he could sense what she was thinking. Maybe he could. Losing their child had sent her reeling with grief and Collin running for the door. Now they were pretending to be a happily married couple ready to restart their family. The irony stung.

Collin pulled into the parking garage of the building where the clinic was located. He turned to her. "Are you ready for this?"

She nodded and opened the door. She had to be. More than one girl's life was at stake.

They took the elevator to the fifth floor. The doctor's name was painted on a door as they stepped off. So far, everything looked respectable. His office was located in a reputable medical center. The waiting room was full of pregnant women and the receptionist greeted them warmly.

Collin asked for a moment of the doctor's time, giving her the cover story they'd created on the drive here. The receptionist agreed to pass along the request and instructed them to take a seat. He led her to a pair of chairs and they sat down. Collin took her hand as her leg jumped nervously.

She glanced at the women surrounding her and tears sprang to her eyes. They'd been in an office like this before only it had been during happier times before they'd lost the baby and he'd left her, when they'd been patients instead of hunting a kidnapper. She glanced around at the women she saw and hoped each of their pregnancies would end happily. Although she was around pregnant teens often, being here with Collin was a painful reminder of what they'd lost.

After a short wait, the receptionist called

their names. "Dr. Rayburn has agreed to see you between patients. Follow me."

She led them down a thickly carpeted hallway. Rebecca noticed state-of-the-art equipment and luxurious furnishings and couldn't help thinking of Missy's description of the girls being held captive in a basement. She doubted they'd had access to such high-tech health care. Had Dr. Rayburn built his wealth by kidnapping women and selling their babies?

The receptionist led them into a private office with the name Jack Rayburn, MD on the door. "He'll be right with you," she said, then closed the door as she left.

Dr. Rayburn arrived moments later. He was tall and lean with thick hair and glasses. "Jack Rayburn. Nice to meet you," he said, shaking both their hands, then taking a seat behind his desk. "My receptionist tells me you two are planning to start a family and are interviewing physicians. Do you have a reason for needing a high-risk obstetrician?"

Collin took the lead. "I'm afraid we haven't been completely honest, Dr. Rayburn. We aren't looking for a physician. We're actually searching for a missing girl." He pulled out a photograph of Missy from before she'd been abducted. "It's my understanding she was one of your patients."

Rayburn glanced at the photograph, then shook his head. "I don't recognize this girl, but I see a lot of patients. I can look up her file if you give me her name."

"Her name is Missy Donovan," Rebecca told him. She couldn't read anything from his expression. Either he was a good actor or he truly didn't recognize her. "We believe she was kidnapped and held captive until she gave birth, then someone sold her baby."

Most people would be shocked to learn about suspected kidnapping and baby selling, but Dr. Rayburn didn't flinch, which struck her as odd. Collin glanced her way, a silent acknowledgment that he'd noticed it too.

Rayburn typed the name into his computer and then shook his head. "I don't have a record of a patient by that name. Who told you I was her doctor?"

Of course there was no file for Missy because she hadn't been an actual patient. "Her boyfriend thought he recognized your name, but it was months ago and he may have been confused."

"I'm sorry I couldn't be of more help."

Collin handed him another photo, this one the security image of the woman who'd tried to kill Rebecca in the hospital. "What about this woman? Do you recognize her?"

He picked up the images and studied them. "It's hard to see. Is this the best image you have? Didn't you photograph her face?"

"No, she kept it hidden from the cameras. We suspect she knew where they were located."

He slid it back across his desk. "I'm sorry. I don't recognize her. Who is she? Is she involved in this baby-selling operation you mentioned?"

"She tried to kill Rebecca at a hospital in Moss Creek."

"How awful." He stood, bringing an end to the meeting. "I'm sorry I can't be more help to you, but I do have to get back to my patients. You remember the way out?"

"We do," Collin said, shaking his hand. "Thank you for your time."

Dr. Rayburn exited the office through one door while Collin opened the one that led back into the hallway.

"Well, that was a bust," he said, and Rebecca was ready to agree with him. The doctor had truly seemed to have no recollection of Missy or the mystery woman who'd attacked her at the hospital. The only odd thing had been his lack of a reaction to his name being linked to a baby-selling operation. It seemed Dylan had either been mistaken in his identification or else he'd intentionally misled them. Talking to him again would be their next step.

They headed down the hallway toward the front office and were nearly to the waiting room when Rebecca spotted a familiar face across the receptionist's desk. Panic filled her and she grabbed Collin's arm.

"What's wrong?" he asked as she dug her fingers into his arm, never removing her eyes from the round face and stocky build of the woman who'd attacked her in the hospital.

"It's her," she told Collin. She pointed at the woman. "It's her. It's the woman that tried to kill me."

Collin glanced to where she indicated and tensed as he recognized the woman from the photo. Although the photo didn't clearly show her face, her hair and build matched. She was even wearing what looked like the same scrubs she had been wearing in the photo. Besides, Rebecca's reaction was all the proof he needed to know it was her.

The woman glanced up and spotted them, scanning both their faces before she turned and disappeared down the hall.

"She saw us," Collin told Rebecca. "And she recognized us. I'm going after her to make sure she doesn't leave the building." He pressed his phone to her. "Call Kent and tell him what's happened. I'll go track her down."

He hurried into the hallway just in time to see the stairwell door swing shut. He glanced through the window, spotted the woman hurrying down and followed her. A posted sign alerted him to the entrance to the parking garage. He couldn't let her get there and into a car or she would get away. He saw her exit through the garage door and followed her.

As he pushed open the door, she swung a large metal object at him, smacking him in the face and propelling him backward. Pain burst through him, sending him to his knees. She tossed the object aside and he realized it was a fire extinguisher.

When he got his bearings again, she was nearing a car. He scrambled to his feet and followed her, but she was already in the car and pulling away by the time he reached her. She hit the accelerator and disappeared before he could follow her.

Rebecca burst through the door and saw him. "Collin, what happened? Where is she?"

"She got away." He slid to the curb and held

his nose, which was bleeding profusely. He couldn't believe he'd let her clock him that way. Amateur move. He stared at Rebecca's face and realized he'd let her down again. "I'm sorry, honey. I'm so sorry."

She kneeled beside him and pulled off her scarf, pressing it against his head to stop the bleeding. "It's not your fault. She may have gotten away, Collin, but now we know who she is. The receptionist gave me her name. It's Joanne Pierson. She's been working for Dr. Rayburn for eight months."

He knew she was right. They were on the right track. This Joanne Pierson had tried to kill Rebecca so she had to be involved in the ring. And she worked for Dr. Rayburn. "He lied when he said he didn't recognize her."

"He had to have known it was her. The photo may not give a good image of her face, but it is definitely her."

He couldn't believe Rayburn had fooled him that way. The man's face had been devoid of recognition. He supposed anyone involved in baby selling would have to be good at hiding his involvement.

And Dylan had been clear that it had been a male doctor who'd snatched Missy. Rayburn was definitely involved.

They'd finally caught a break in the case.

* * *

Collin and Rebecca made a report at the police department in the jurisdiction where the medical center was located. Kent phoned them ahead of time to alert them about the situation they were currently investigating and he arrived an hour later as Collin and Rebecca were finishing up giving their statements.

"How sure are you that it was her?" Kent asked Rebecca.

She didn't hesitate. She would never forget that face or the contempt in her words. *You should have listened to our warnings. Now, you'll go to sleep and never wake up.* "It was her."

"She ran when she saw Rebecca," Collin reminded him. "That should be enough to confirm Rebecca's story."

Kent pulled out the photographs the hospital's camera had captured of the woman and compared it to her hospital credentials the office had provided for Joanne Pierson. "It certainly could be her," he said. "I ran her history. She's never been arrested, but she was a person of interest in a kidnapping in Alabama. A two-year-old boy went missing two days after the mother took him to his pediatrician. Pierson was working at the office.

The mother chatted with her during the visit and stated she seemed very interested in the boy. The day he disappeared, the mother recalled seeing Pierson in the parking lot of the store where he vanished. The locals couldn't prove she was involved and she left town before they could question her. Before that job at the pediatrician's office, there's no record of her. We checked out the last known address she had, but it was either too old or a fake. She also doesn't have a car registered in her name. All this leads me to believe that Pierson is most likely a faked identity."

"That makes sense," Collin said. "What about Rayburn?"

"I've contacted Dr. Rayburn but he's refusing to cooperate. He claims you lied your way into his office then caused a commotion that affected his business and frightened his patients. He denied having any involvement in a baby-selling ring."

Collin couldn't deny they'd lied and that they'd caused a commotion, but under the circumstances, they'd been justified. "He lied to us about knowing his own nurse, Kent. If he lied about that, he must have lied about Missy, too. I think he knew exactly who we were talking about."

"Maybe. I'll do some digging into his background to see if we can find anything that might indicate his involvement. It's possible he hired this nurse with no knowledge of what she was doing. An OB nurse could be useful to the operation just like a doctor."

Rebecca shook her head. "No. Dylan said a male doctor abducted Missy, not a nurse or a woman. He was very specific. Plus, he identified Rayburn as the man he'd seen."

"He might have been lying," Kent suggested.

Collin shook his head, agreeing with Rebecca. "He isn't sophisticated enough to give us just enough to lead us here but mislead us on other things. He's just a scared kid, Kent. Rayburn is involved. I know he is. Now, we just have to prove it."

Kent packed up his papers. "I'll swing by the hospital and see if I can interview some of the staff on the OB floor. Maybe other medical personnel who've worked with him will have something different to say about him and his practices."

Rebecca stood. "Thank you, Kent."

"I'm only doing my job, Rebecca. I'll collect as much evidence as I can until the FBI arrive to take over."

"I know, but I'm grateful you're on our side."

He seemed pleased by her words but then

his expression darkened. "We haven't found any evidence that points to a dirty cop being involved in this. Is it possible Missy was mistaken?"

"Anything is possible, but she was scared and so certain."

"Well, I've had one of my most trusted officers looking into it, but whoever it was Missy saw could also have come from one of the other local police agencies or sheriff's offices around. In fact, given the location of the warehouse being so far from Moss Creek, it's more likely."

"I know you're right," she told him.

He nodded. "I'll see you two back in Moss Creek."

Rebecca watched him go and realized he was another person she was slowly learning to trust. She was glad she'd taken a chance on him.

Collin couldn't get Dylan's words from his mind.

How can I take care of a baby?

I'm not ready for that responsibility.

What about my life?

He recalled having the same questions when Rebecca had told him about their pregnancy. He'd had no one there, no male figure to reassure him that everything was going to be okay. He'd realized last night after the talk with Rebecca that he could be that person for Dylan, if not about the baby then about other important life matters. Despite what he'd done, he was still just a scared kid who needed guidance if he had any shot of becoming a man who mattered.

After taking Rebecca back to her father's house, he drove to the jail and asked to see Dylan. A deputy led him into a long corridor that housed the holding cells. Collin had already spoken to the public defender and the prosecutor about not charging him in covering up the abduction in exchange for helping them find the people behind this baby-selling ring. It was at least some good news he could share with the boy.

The deputy led him through the gated door and motioned toward the last unit before he closed the door behind Collin. He glanced at the empty holding cells near the front and found it odd that Dylan had been placed in the last cell, farthest away from the guards. He would speak to Kent about having him moved so he didn't seem so isolated.

He approached the last door and spotted Dylan even before he made it all the way to the end of the corridor. The boy was hanging from a noose and he wasn't moving.

"Dylan! Help!" Collin hollered back to the gate. "Someone help!" The deputy appeared at the gate. "Open the cell. Open the cell!"

He ran toward them, spotted Dylan and quickly unlocked the cell door. Collin hurried inside, grabbed Dylan and tried to hold him up while the deputy climbed onto the bed and untied him.

Collin lowered the boy to the ground and checked for a pulse. It was faint. "He's alive. Call for an ambulance."

The deputy nodded and radioed in the request.

Collin untied the noose from around Dylan's neck and saw the bruises. He cried out to God. Why had He allowed this? Why hadn't someone been watching Dylan more closely?

He should have heeded the calling to help Dylan before now. He should have known how the boy was feeling, the despair of knowing he'd messed up and caused a person he cared about pain. Collin shook his head. He'd failed this boy just as surely as he'd failed Rebecca.

As the paramedics arrived, so did Kent. He approached Collin. "What happened?"

"He tried to hang himself. Why was he in here all alone?'

"According to the report, he wasn't deemed a suicide risk."

"He's just a kid!" Collin felt his insides constrict. If he'd been here earlier, this might not have happened. Anger bit through him. It wasn't right. It wasn't fair. He should have been able to stop it, to help Dylan. That's what he'd come for and that's what he should have told the boy when he first saw him. Instead, he'd allowed him to be placed alone, seemingly forgotten, with nothing but his failures to mull over.

He stayed with Dylan until the paramedics arrived and transported him to the hospital.

"We'll order an official investigation," Kent told him. "We'll find out what happened here."

But Collin knew what had happened. He'd failed yet another person he was meant to protect.

Rebecca was waiting for Collin in the garage when he arrived back at the house. Kent had phoned to let her know what had happened to Dylan and that Collin was taking the blow hard.

She saw it, too, in the way his shoulders

slumped as he got out of his car. Those shoulders had seen so much pain and had tried to carry it all.

She walked to him and hugged him, wrapping her arms tightly around him, and he enveloped her before digging his head into her shoulder.

"One thing you learn working with these kids, Collin, is that you can't solve everyone's problem. I learned that lesson a long time ago. You need to learn it, too."

"What are you talking about? They were *our* problems."

She realized they'd slipped back to talking about the past. "And we should have solved them together."

"We needed something, Rebecca, something I couldn't give you. I didn't know where to turn or what to do back then. I needed help."

"I never asked you to give me anything. It's always been in your nature to want to fix everything, but some things are just broken. It's the world we live in. If you could fix everything, we would never need Jesus."

She'd left everything for him and in his mind, he'd believed he had to fix that, to make up for the sacrifice she'd made to be with him. But she'd never asked him to do that and never wanted to be fixed.

"Love isn't really love without sacrifice, is it? Jesus made the ultimate sacrifice to save our souls. I gave up money and comfort to be with the man I loved and you know what, Collin? It wasn't even that much of a sacrifice because I never cared about those things. I know I had a lot of growing up to do back then. I confess, it was sort of a culture shock and I wasn't as enlightened as I liked to believe. It was hard for me to live that way, to struggle. I was spoiled by the life I grew up in, but that wasn't your fault and it wasn't something you needed to fix."

"If I'd been a better provider, the baby—"

"The baby was not your fault, Collin. There was nothing you could have done. It happened. I cried for our loss but it never affected my decision to be with you. Maybe we got married because I was pregnant, but it was always in my plan to be your wife. Always." She touched his face and stared deeply into his eyes. The pain welling deep inside of him burst and she took him into her arms. How foolish it was that they'd lost so many years because of something as silly as money and pride. But it hadn't been silly to him. It had been a real struggle that she hadn't even realized he was having. She'd been so caught up in her own grief that she hadn't noticed his anguish.

He touched her cheek and the expression on his face stunned her. For years, she'd longed to see him look at her that way again. Attraction. Need. Love. "You are so beautiful," he told her, his finger stroking her face, sending waves of emotion fluttering through her. "I've loved you for my entire life, Rebecca, and, in case I haven't said it recently, I'm so sorry. I was a fool to ever let you go."

She stared up into his eyes. Yes, he'd been foolish, but hadn't they both been? They'd been too young and too inexperienced for the problems that had been thrown at them, but in his arms was where she had always wanted to be. She still did. It didn't erase the grief she'd suffered at his abandonment, but she was finally ready to put that pain behind her and move forward. She smiled up at him. "Don't foolish people sometimes learn from their mistakes?"

He breathed in deeply and placed his other hand on her cheek. "I sure have."

"Then stop talking about it and kiss me."

She'd spent years dreaming of his kiss, remembering the feel of his lips against hers and the weight of his arms around her, but her memory was a shell of the real thing. She leaned into him and suddenly it was as if they had never been apart.

She never wanted to be anywhere else.

EIGHT

Rebecca checked her hair in the mirror before she went downstairs. She smiled at the thought of seeing Collin. It felt silly to her to get so excited about seeing him at breakfast, but after their kiss last night, she knew she wanted to see him at breakfast every morning for the rest of her life.

She fingered the ring on her necklace. It might not be long until it was back on her finger for good, something she'd only dared to dream about in the years they'd spent apart. Now, her future looked bright again. It was a scary feeling to even hope for something like this with Collin, but it was a good kind of scary and a risk she was willing to take.

"Someone had a good night."

She spun from the mirror and saw Janice standing in her doorway, a knowing smile on her face.

Rebecca felt her face redden but she pushed

aside her embarrassment. She was happy. And it was time. She'd only just *existed* for too long. A big, silly grin spread across her face and she suddenly felt like a teenager. "I did."

Janice walked in and closed the door. "Do tell."

"He kissed me, Jan. Last night, Collin kissed me, and it was exactly like what I remembered, but different. Like a man's kiss now."

"I saw this coming."

"You did?"

She nodded. "When I saw Collin at the hospital that day, I told David later that you two would be back together in no time. You've always been in love with him, at least ever since I can remember. That's why you've never dated or gotten married, isn't it? You never got over him?"

"No, I guess I never did."

Janice pulled her into a hug. "I'm glad to see you happy again, coz. I've always wanted the best for you. That's why I tried to set you up all those times with friends of David, even though you rejected everyone. Now, I know it wasn't them."

"They were all very nice guys, but they—"

"Weren't Collin Walsh," Janice said, finishing for her.

Rebecca could only nod. That was exactly the problem. Even if she hadn't been married, and therefore unable to get serious about any one of the men Janice had tried to fix her up with, not one of them had measured up to Collin. Despite how he'd hurt her, her heart had always belonged to him.

Janice took her arm. "Well, let's go downstairs to breakfast. I suppose if you're willing to give this man a second chance, there must be something redeeming about him. I'm willing to try to find it, too."

"Thanks, Jan."

"Don't thank me. I may be willing to suspend my annoyance at the way this man broke your heart, but I doubt your father will be as forgiving."

Rebecca hurried downstairs, but knew Janice was right. Her father had never approved of Collin, but that hadn't stopped Rebecca from falling for him twelve years ago, and it wouldn't stop her now, either.

They entered the dining room to find her father already seated and feeding Matthew, whose high chair was pushed up to the table.

"Uncle Bobby, you didn't have to feed him. I was going to do that," Janice told him.

"Nonsense. I'm enjoying the time we've been spending together. I'll be sad to see you two heading back to your house."

Janice sighed, then sat down and poured herself a glass of orange juice. "I think Matthew has enjoyed it, too, but David will be home this afternoon and I can't wait to be sleeping back in my own bed."

"That was once your bed," her father reminded Janice.

She laughed it off. "You know what I mean, Uncle Bobby."

Rebecca took a chair and watched the interaction between her dad and Matthew. The baby seemed to bring out the best in her father. She wondered how he would have been with his own grandchild. Would they have spent time together? Gone to ball games? A wave of sadness washed over her. She would never know and she'd accepted that a long time ago. At least, she thought she had, but losing a child had changed her forever and it seemed wrong to keep such grief to herself. She'd hidden it for so many years, kept it tightly inside her for fear of forgetting. But now it struck her as wrong that she'd denied her family from knowing about her baby.

She watched her father now playing with Matthew and for the first time in a long while had hope that there would be other children, his own grandchildren, for him to love. She was glad the cloud of suspicion was gone and she could trust him again. He really was a good man and had been a good father. A little overindulgent, perhaps, but who could blame him for that? She'd had to grow up fast, but that had been her choice, not his, and he'd welcomed her back home without a hint of condemnation for her actions. If she was being truthful, she hadn't told him about marrying Collin or about the baby partly because she hadn't wanted to let him down again. But keeping that secret had turned to resentment and bitterness a long time ago. She'd had no one to share her pain and grief and it had erected a wall around her heart.

Her heart jumped as Collin walked into the room. His hair was still damp from his shower and his smile was as big as hers as he took the chair beside her.

"Good morning," he said, his eyes locking with Rebecca's, and she felt herself blush as she remembered the feel of his lips on hers.

"Good morning," she replied.

"Good grief," her father said, his tone reflecting his annoyance at this development. "I'm having lunch at the club this afternoon, Rebecca. Why don't you join me? Mrs. Banks has been wanting to speak with you about the end-of-summer banquet. Remember you promised to help her organize it." He glanced at Collin. "There's plenty of security so she should be safe there, but you're welcome to come, too, if that would make Rebecca feel safer."

Rebecca smiled, knowing how extending that invitation to Collin had to hurt her father. But she had other plans for the day. "I can't today, Dad. I have court tomorrow and I can't miss it so I asked my office to messenger over the case files on the court's docket. I need to spend the day going through them and preparing my recommendations."

"I'd be happy to help Mrs. Banks with the banquet," Janice interjected. She stood and wiped Matthew's face then picked him up.

"I think Mrs. Banks would like that. Thank you, Janice."

They got up and left the room, leaving Rebecca alone with Collin. He reached for her hand and kissed it, then leaned over and kissed her, too.

"I don't think your dad is very happy about what's happening here."

"He never was." She smiled and leaned into him. "But I'm happy."

"So am I."

She thought she could live in his eyes but they still had more pressing things than being lovey-dovey all day long.

"So you're working all day," he said as he bit into a piece of dry toast.

She nodded. "I have a lot of recommendations to write. You know how important my job is to me. I can't let these kids down." She pointed a finger at him. "And don't you tell me it's too dangerous for me to go to court because I'm going."

"I know. It's okay. I need to call the Realtor back about my mom's house. He's left me three voice mails that have gone unanswered."

She'd nearly forgotten that was why he'd come to town.

"I also want to check in on Dylan."

"You have things to do and so do I. It's going to be a long and boring day, isn't it?"

He smiled and stood before placing a kiss on her lips. "It is, but it'll be a safe day. I'm glad we're staying inside for once. I'm going to make my calls. I'll check on you in a while."

She watched him walk out and resisted the urge to sigh. She had no right to be this happy when her life was in danger and Missy was still missing. But she was.

She walked into the kitchen and found the box containing her files and a borrowed laptop from one of her colleagues. Janice was there now, too, pouring apple juice into a bottle for Matthew.

"I was just preparing a bag for Lily, our nanny. She's coming by to pick up Matthew while I go to the club with Uncle Bobby."

"Thank you for taking over that banquet, Janice. It's never been something I enjoyed."

"I'm glad to do it. I enjoy spending time with your dad, although it's you he really wants to spend time with. I'm his second choice."

"You've never been second choice, Janice. Dad loves having you here and I can see he's enjoying spending so much time with Matthew." The bruises on her cousin's face were a reminder of what she'd endured because of Rebecca, because of her investigation. It pained her to see someone she cared about injured and she couldn't even think about what might have happened to Matthew if he'd been with her. "I only wish there wasn't so much bickering. I wish Collin and Dad could get along better."

"They're both protecting something they love," Janice said. "It makes sense. When your father first took me in when I was a kid, I know you and Collin grew exasperated when I wanted to spend time with you, but I looked up to you both. I always thought you were the perfect couple. You were so beautiful and funny, and Collin was handsome and athletic. I thought you were like Romeo and Juliet."

Rebecca didn't care for that comparison. "Janice, they killed themselves."

"I'm not expressing myself well. Rebecca, I love that we've grown closer as we've both gotten older. You've never shared what happened with you and Collin when you ran away together but I remember you were so sad when you returned. You'd lost that carefree light about you. You were never the same afterward. I didn't understand it then because I thought he loved you so much. How could he leave you that way? It broke my heart, too, to learn he was only after the money."

Rebecca stopped and turned to her. "What money? What are you talking about?"

"The money your dad paid him to leave you."

Rebecca sat down, fearful she would shatter as the world seemed to open up and swallow her. What on earth was her cousin talking about? "Wh-what?'

Janice's eyes widened and she pressed

her hand to her mouth. "You didn't know? I shouldn't have said anything." She gathered up Matthew and started to leave but Rebecca met her around the table and stopped her.

"What are you talking about? Collin took money from my father?"

Her face said she didn't want to tell her so Rebecca knew it was bad. She bounced Matthew on her hip as she stared at Rebecca. "I overheard your parents fighting. Collin phoned your dad wanting money. He said he would disappear and never bother you again if your dad paid him ten thousand dollars."

Rebecca felt her heart seem to stop and suddenly she had trouble catching her breath. It wasn't true. It wasn't true. It wasn't true. "Ten thousand dollars?" Was that all their relationship, their marriage, their child, had meant to him? Ten thousand dollars?

"It doesn't seem like much money now but I imagine to a broke young man, it must have seemed like a fortune."

She grabbed Janice's arm. "Why were my parents fighting?"

"Your mom didn't want to pay him a dime but your dad said he would pay any price to get you back." Matthew fussed in her arms. "I'd better go tend to him." She reached out to Rebecca's arm. "I'm sorry. I thought you knew."

Once she was gone, Rebecca slid back into a chair at the table. She was still dumbfounded by this whole new betrayal. And she couldn't believe her father had never told her about the money. He could have broken her tie to Collin permanently if he'd wanted. Then why hadn't he?

Tears sprung to her eyes. She'd never suspected Collin would take money from her father. Never. He'd been the one person in her life who didn't care about the money. Or so she'd thought. Just yesterday he'd been telling her how he'd struggled to support her. Had it been because he'd been expecting to live off her father while they were married? He'd expected to marry an heiress and ended up with a pauper?

She forced her legs to work and headed for the living room, where Collin was finishing up a call. He turned and smiled when he saw her and her heart broke. Was he after more money now? Had she been wrong about him from the start? She had to know the truth.

He touched her arm and she pulled it away. She couldn't afford to get sucked back into his charm and strength. No matter how much she wanted to fall into his arms, she couldn't. She had to remember how he'd betrayed her. For years, she'd blamed herself for his leaving. That she wasn't good enough. Now, she knew the truth. He'd been hoping to cash in on their relationship.

"What's wrong?" he asked when she pulled away.

Rebecca spotted her father walking into the room. She didn't want to do this with an audience, but she couldn't leave until she knew the truth. Had the two most important men in her life conspired to betray her? She knew why her father would do such a thing. He would have done anything to keep her and Collin apart. But why would Collin betray her this way? It was time everything was out in the open.

She turned back to Collin, doing her best to keep her voice flat so the sobs that threatened her wouldn't break through and turn her into a sniveling mess. "Twelve years ago, did you take money from my father to leave me?"

He looked at her, surprise filling out his expression. "What? What are you talking about?"

"Twelve years ago, after I lost the baby, did you take money from my father to leave me and not return?"

"Baby?" her father gasped from behind her. She ignored him for now. She would deal with him later.

She saw the truth on Collin's face as his smile vanished and he turned away from her. Her heart broke. Had he denied it, she might have believed it was all a big lie or a misunderstanding. But it was true. It was all true.

"It's not what you think," he finally said.

"You took money from my father to leave me. It's exactly like it sounds." Her chin quivered and tears pooled in her eyes but she choked them back. She couldn't fall apart now. "Is that why you married me? Because you wanted the money?"

Her father gasped again. "Married you? Rebecca, what did you do?"

Again, she ignored his question.

Collin stepped toward her. "No, Rebecca, it wasn't like that." He reached for her arms and she jerked them away.

"I thought you were different, Collin. I thought you didn't care about any of this."

"I only cared about you. After we lost the baby, I got so scared. I didn't know what to do. I couldn't function. I realized I couldn't care for you and there were all these bills to pay. People wanting their money. I didn't want to lose you, but I convinced myself you would be better off without me. I called your father and he came and took you home."

"It's bad enough you left me but you took money to do it?"

"The money was for the hospital bills. For the baby."

She was well aware of her father standing behind them, shocked by the mention of the baby as well as the marriage. She didn't care. It was time to come clean about everything. But she was through listening to excuses. "So you took a payoff to abandon your own wife? If you'd wanted out so badly you could have just told me. You didn't have to go behind my back."

"I didn't want out. That was the last thing I wanted. But I couldn't protect you. I couldn't care for you or our child. I couldn't even keep the lights on most of the time."

"Then we should have handled it together. I've spent the past twelve years blaming myself and when I saw you again, I wondered if I could ever really trust you again. You had me fooled, Collin, because I was trusting you again. For the first time in a long, long time, I was looking forward to the future again. It was bad enough that you left me but to discover it was all about the money… That's a betrayal I can never forgive."

"Rebecca, please."

She put up her hands as he tried to reach

out to her. She didn't even want to be in the same room with him, much less the same house. "I—I can't even look at you anymore. I don't want to see you again. I want you to leave."

"You need me here. Your life is still in danger."

"It doesn't matter. I can't trust you. I'll never trust you again. I will hire someone to keep me safe. At least I'll know where I stand with him. Goodbye, Collin."

He stepped away from her, dug his hands into his pockets and gave a heavy sigh. The pain on his face only made her even more angry. How dare he pretend to be hurt when she was the one devastated by his betrayal.

"I'm sorry I hurt you," he said before he walked out.

She didn't move until she heard the slamming of the front door, then she burst into tears. Her father stepped toward her, intending probably to comfort her, but she didn't want his pity, either.

She ran upstairs to her childhood bedroom for a long overdue cry.

Collin tossed his suitcase into the back seat of his rental car then got in, slamming the door hard. He had no idea how things had fallen apart so fast. An hour ago, he'd been hopeful for a future with Rebecca. Now, he knew that would never happen. He'd lost her for a second time and, like the first, it was all his fault. He hadn't been honest with her. When she'd confronted him about the money he'd taken from her father, he'd tried to justify his actions, believing she could never love him if she knew the truth. But, as usual, she'd seen right through his excuses.

The truth was he'd wanted something he could never have. He'd reached for Rebecca and had fallen short, but money had seemed to make everything better for those who had it. He'd hoped it would make it all better for him, too. It hadn't. It had made him a coward, too afraid to face his own issues. The army had taught him to confront situations head-on and never flinch, and he could do that when it was a physical confrontation. He was good at that. He was well trained to disarm a gunman or guard a base from enemy attack. But he'd never learned to fight the battles of the heart, issues that couldn't be fixed with a gun or proper perimeter defense.

He also knew something else. He'd never faced the consequences of his decision to take that money and run. He'd left Rebecca to face the mess he'd made alone. He was glad she hadn't lived the past twelve years knowing he'd left her because of the money. That would have been too heartbreaking for her. But she knew it now and she was hurting and he realized that, once again, he'd tried to justify his way out of the problem instead of taking responsibility for his actions and apologizing.

Yes, he'd been a frightened kid in over his head. But he'd also been a husband and father, and his wife had deserved better than what he'd given her. She'd deserved the truth. It was time he learned. Rebecca may never forgive him and probably would never consider a future with him again, but he could face this problem and give her the proper apology she deserved.

He pulled out a notebook and jotted down some notes. This was also a good life lesson he could pass on to Dylan, assuming the boy survived his injuries. The last update Collin had heard was that he was still unconscious.

He stared up at Rebecca's window and saw the curtains were drawn. She didn't want to see him. His instinct was to sit outside to make sure she was safe. But there was little he could do if she didn't want him around.

He phoned Kent and wasn't surprised to find him at the sheriff's office. "I need a favor. Can you increase patrols around Bob Mason's house?"

"Is there a problem? Has something happened?"

There was a big problem and something had definitely happened, but he wasn't interested in going into it with Kent. "Rebecca and I had a fight and she asked me to leave. She's planning to hire a bodyguard, but I would appreciate some extra security for the house for the next day or so."

"No problem. I'll take care of it," Kent said.

"Thank you. I was thinking of swinging by the hospital to see Dylan. Have you gotten any updates on him?"

"Not on his condition, but I did place a guard on his door in case someone wanted to keep him from waking up. I found something disturbing during my check of the cameras around the holding cells. One of my deputies, John Seaver, was the last one to log in to the holding area before Dylan was found hanging. He should have had no reason to be there. He wasn't even on duty."

That was interesting. Had he said something to Dylan to make the kid want to hang himself? Or had he tied the rope himself, going back to the dirty-cop scenario? "Is there any reason to suspect he might have done something to Dylan?"

"There was one thing. Right after Seaver logged in, the cameras in the holding cells went dark. They came back on once he was gone and it was only a few minutes later that you arrived and found Dylan."

Collin shook his head and sighed. If he hadn't shown up, Deputy Seaver might have succeeded in killing the boy. It was looking more and more like Missy had been right about a dirty cop.

"It's too early to say what did or didn't happen during that time, especially since we can't talk to Dylan yet, but I'm bringing Seaver in for questioning. He has a lot of explaining to do about why he was there."

Collin would like to have been there to hear those answers, but his gut told him they would only be lies. His time was better served going to the hospital and making certain Dylan knew he had people around who cared about him. "Let me know what he says. And thanks for the extra patrols, Kent."

"No problem. I'll call you later."

Collin drove to the hospital and parked, then walked up to the third floor, where a nurse showed him to Dylan's room.

"How is he doing?" he asked her and she gave him a reassuring smile.

"He regained consciousness a while ago and he's going to be fine. No permanent damage."

That was good news. He approached Dylan's room and slipped inside. The kid was asleep but the machines beside his bed continued to monitor his vitals. Collin stared at the ugly marks on his neck and grimaced, but also noticed bruises on his arms as well. Had those been there before? He didn't think so.

Dylan opened his eyes and looked his way as Collin approached the bed.

"Hey, Dylan. How are you feeling? I came to check on you. To see how you are."

His voice was scratchy from the swelling and he seemed groggy, but he got right to the point. "I didn't do it, Mr. Walsh," the boy said adamantly. "I didn't try to kill myself like they're saying."

"I found you hanging from the neck, Dylan. Can you tell me what happened in that cell?"

"Someone was there. I didn't know him but he grabbed me. I blacked out. That's the last thing I remember until I woke up here and the nurse said I'd tried to commit suicide. It's not true, Mr. Walsh. I didn't do that."

Collin moved closer to the bed and pulled up a chair. "Can you describe this man, Dylan?"

"I'm not sure. It all happened so quick, but I know he was wearing a uniform. He was one of the deputies at the jail."

As the kid drifted to sleep again, Collin pulled out his phone and texted this new information to Kent. He would need that information when he questioned this Deputy Seaver about why he was at the jail.

Kent definitely had a rogue deputy on his hands and would have to add security around Dylan. If this deputy had been working on the ring's orders to shut Dylan up, the kid wasn't safe.

He pulled out his phone again to call Rebecca to update her on Dylan's condition, but the call went straight to her voice mail. He imagined she'd seen the caller ID and let it roll over, not wanting to speak to him. He couldn't blame her. It had barely been an hour since their blowup. He left a short message, letting her know the boy was going to be fine, then ended the call. He would try calling her again later or going over there. Whatever he had to do, whether she ever spoke to him again or not, he wasn't giving up on keeping her safe.

He would protect her with his last breath.

* * *

Rebecca packed her bag and left with Janice and David when he arrived to pick up his family. As she sat in the back of their SUV, she couldn't help but think how quickly her life had gone downhill. She was right back where she'd started, alone and in danger. Her heart longed for Collin and the bright future she'd already started imagining, but how would she ever trust Collin or her father again? They'd both betrayed her in terrible ways. Her father for offering the man she loved money to leave her...and Collin for accepting it. It was a blow she wasn't sure she could ever get past.

She thanked her cousin again for allowing her to stay, then carried her bag upstairs, along with the box of her files, and locked herself into the spare bedroom. Her cheeks were wet with tears when a knock came on the door and she heard Janice's voice call her name. She quickly wiped away the tears and unlocked the door. Janice stood in the hall carrying a tray with a plate of food and a glass of sweet tea.

"I brought you some supper and before you say you're not hungry, you have to eat something."

She smiled. She had been about to say those

very words. Janice knew her so well. "Thank you," she said instead, taking the tray.

Janice walked into the room and closed the door. "You look terrible."

"Thank you."

"No, I mean it, Rebecca. I've never seen you look like this before, not since…well, not since the last time with Collin. You two must have had quite the falling-out this time."

The final falling-out. "We did."

She walked into the adjoining bathroom, turned on the faucet and ran a washcloth under the water. "Well, it's a good thing you found this out now before things got too serious between the two of you." She handed the washcloth to Rebecca, who could only laugh at that statement.

"I'd say things were very serious."

"I know you care about him, Rebecca. I'm just saying it's a good thing you found this out before you married the man."

She got up and went to the bathroom again. "I did marry him," Rebecca said. Now that her father knew her secret, it was time everyone else did, too. "We also had a baby."

At first, Janice didn't seem to hear her. She laughed then ran another washcloth under the sink. After a moment, she turned to Rebecca. "Wait, what?" She took up a stance in the doorway. "What do you mean you married him?"

Rebecca nodded as she wiped away the tears. "Collin and I are married."

She looked stunned. "I knew you were falling hard for him, Becca, but I had no idea you were in this deep."

"I married Collin twelve years ago when we ran off together. We got married by a justice of the peace in Louisiana."

Janice gasped. "Because of the baby?"

"Yes. We ran off together when I discovered I was pregnant."

"And you never told anyone? Your dad didn't know?"

She shook her head. "We weren't trying to hide it. I just thought once the baby was born, he would see his grandchild and everything would be forgiven." She lowered her head at the memory of that terrible loss. "That obviously didn't happen. I lost the baby and soon after Collin left."

Janice pulled her into a hug. "No wonder you were such a wreck. I'm so sorry, Rebecca. I had no idea."

"I was too ashamed to tell anyone. Part of me kept hoping he would come back but another part knew he wasn't. I had no idea how to go about getting a divorce from him and I wasn't about to tell Daddy what I'd done."

"He would have been furious that you'd gotten married, but he would have helped you."

She nodded. "He would have constantly reminded me how he was right about Collin. I just didn't want to hear that. It was easier just to pick up my life and move on. By the time, I was old enough and knew enough about the world to get a divorce, I was too embarrassed. I had no idea where Collin was and without him there to sign the papers, I would have had to place an ad in the paper. I just couldn't do it."

Janice hugged her again. "Well, you know where he is now. We can get this all straightened out before he skips town again. And I'll go with you to see a lawyer."

"He's not going to skip town, Janice, but thank you. I suppose it is time to put an end to this marriage once and for all."

"He left you once, Rebecca. What makes you think he won't do it again?"

She opened her mouth to make excuses for him, all the ones he'd given for himself. He'd been a scared teenager with no prospects—but it sounded hollow even to her own mind. Janice had just asked the same question she'd been struggling with ever since Collin reappeared in her life. How did she know he wouldn't leave her again? She sighed at the truth. She didn't. If today's encounter had proven anything to her, it was that she didn't really know Collin. She'd seen him through lovestruck youthful eyes, but she wasn't a child anymore and she couldn't put her faith in someone who was going to let her down again. She couldn't take that heartbreak again.

"I'll let you get some rest," Janice said. "You should try to sleep. Everything will look clearer tomorrow."

She watched Janice walk out then crawled under the blankets and sobbed into her pillow. She might not be able to trust Collin, but that didn't stop her heart from wanting him.

Rebecca awoke the next morning and went downstairs. The sun was shining outside, but she didn't feel particularly cheery. She had court at 2:00 p.m. and she still had recommendations to write. Plus, she had the added task of hiring someone to act as a bodyguard for her now that she'd vowed never to see Collin again. And the FBI was supposed to be coming into town. They would want to question Rebecca at some point. Her life was booked and the things she needed to do didn't stop because she was brokenhearted.

Matthew was in his high chair nibbling a biscuit when she entered the kitchen. Janice was at the stove cooking.

"How did you sleep?" her cousin asked and Rebecca only shrugged.

She'd had a difficult time falling asleep. Thoughts of Collin kept moving through her head. The good times together and the bad. Even when everything around them had been falling apart, after the baby's death and the bills and no money, she'd still been happy with him. He'd always been everything she'd wanted and needed. It stung to know he'd thought so little of her that a few thousand dollars could alter his devotion to her, especially when she'd given up everything to be with him.

Her cousin handed her a plate of eggs and toast, but Rebecca only picked at her food. She wasn't hungry.

Janice obviously saw how down she was. "I'm sure it will all work out," she said. She unbuckled the baby from his high chair. "This little guy has been up for hours. I'm going to try to put him down for an early nap, then we'll talk."

After Janice left the room, Rebecca carried

her plate to the sink and emptied her food into the disposal. She washed the plate and set it in the rack by the sink. The refrigerator was covered in photos of Janice, David and baby Matthew. He was such a bright boy and Rebecca smiled at his photos. Her eyes scanned the refrigerator, noting cards and daily planners for diet, exercise and appointments. Janice was organized to the point of obsession.

Rebecca saw a note on the calendar and an appointment card attached with Janice's name on the card. It was for a doctor's appointment with Dr. Rayburn. She gasped. She didn't know her cousin was a patient of Dr. Rayburn, and after what she suspected she knew about the man, she hated to believe her cousin would see him. She had to tell Janice her suspicions of Rayburn and pray she found another physician.

But something about the photo of Matthew with David and Janice sent a terrible thought rustling through her. Janice had tried for years to get pregnant before finally adopting little Matthew. But now that Rebecca knew about the baby-selling ring operating around town, was it possible the child her cousin had adopted had come from there?

No, she refused to believe Janice would be involved in something like that. Just because

Matthew was adopted did not mean he came from the ring. Janice walked back into the kitchen and Rebecca debated whether or not to speak. But she needed to know for certain.

Her cousin glanced at her curiously. "You've got that crazy-eyes look, Rebecca. Is something wrong?"

She turned to her and held out the appointment card. "Dr. Rayburn is your doctor?"

"Yes, he is."

"Janice, did he have a hand in helping you adopt Matthew?"

Janice gave her a hard look. "What's going on, Rebecca?"

"He's a bad man, Janice. Collin and I believe he's involved in kidnapping women and stealing their babies. Please tell me you didn't get Matthew through him. Please tell me he didn't have a hand in his adoption."

"That's ridiculous. Dr. Rayburn is a well-known obstetrician. He wouldn't be involved in anything like that."

Rebecca noted her cousin hadn't answered her question. She didn't really have to. Rebecca saw fear simmering beneath her expression. Fear that her child might have been stolen and could thus be taken from her. Fear of losing her child. Rebecca shared her fear but she wouldn't allow it to stop her from doing the right thing.

"You're being ridiculous," Janice told her. She turned her back and began picking up toys from the floor.

"He's a monster, Janice. We have to do something. Tell me, how did he find Matthew? What attorney did you use?"

Janice turned to her, tears pooling in her eyes. She placed the toys in her arms onto the side table then leaned against it for support. "No," she cried, her own anguish evident. "This cannot be happening."

"We need to go to the police. If we can backtrack Matthew's adoption, we would finally have evidence linking Rayburn to the baby-selling ring." She reached for her phone on the bar and started dialing Kent's number. She was excited to finally have a break in the case but, as she glanced at Janice still leaning against the table, she was saddened at the personal costs of this case. She couldn't believe she hadn't put it all together sooner.

She hadn't even finished dialing when a guttural scream erupted from her cousin. Janice grabbed the lamp from the table and lunged for her as Rebecca spun to face her. Pain shot through her as Janice hit her. The room spun and her knees buckled. She managed to glance at Janice and saw her eyes on fire with anger as she swung the lamp again, hitting Rebecca and sending her to the floor, where darkness quickly pulled her away.

NINE

Pain ripped through Rebecca's head as she regained consciousness. She groaned then remembered Janice attacking her. What was that about? She tried to lift her hand to her aching head and discovered she couldn't. Her hands were bound behind her back. She opened her eyes and pain sliced through her head at the light flowing inside from the curtains. Something wet and warm was on her face. Blood, she assumed, from where Janice had smacked her.

She glanced around and saw Janice sitting on the couch. She was biting her nails and looked like she was about to lose control.

"What happened?" Rebecca asked, realizing she was tied up with duct tape. What was going on and why had her cousin attacked her?

"Shut up," Janice told her as she stood up

and began pacing. She checked her phone. "Where are you, David?"

"Janice, why am I tied up? What's going on? Why are you doing this?

Janice spun on her, her expression full of anger and contempt. "You're trying to take my baby from me."

"No, no. I wasn't. But if Dr. Rayburn was involved in your adoption, Matthew might have been stolen from his real mother."

"I'm his real mother," she shrieked. "And you're not going to take him from me!"

The back door slammed and Rebecca heard David's voice calling out for his wife. "Janice, I got your message. What's going on?" He followed her glance down to Rebecca and he paled. "What have you done, Janice?"

Rebecca was relieved to see him. If anyone could calm down Janice and make her see reason, it was him.

"She was going to call the police. She was trying to take Matthew."

"I wasn't," Rebecca insisted. "I just wanted to know if Dr. Rayburn was connected to Matthew. He's a bad man, David. He kidnapped a girl and stole her baby from her."

David kneeled beside Rebecca. "I know all about your investigation, Rebecca. Why couldn't you just leave things alone?"

A sick feeling rolled through her at the coldness in David's face. He wasn't there to help her or calm down his wife. She glanced up at her cousin. They were practically sisters. She couldn't believe Janice could be involved with Rayburn. Tears filled her eyes. David and Janice had stolen Matthew away from a woman held captive and they'd both done it with open eyes.

"What are you going to do with me?"

He shrugged. "As long as you're alive, you're a danger to our operation."

"Our operation? So you didn't just get Matthew from Rayburn? You're working with him, too?" This was so much worse than she'd initially thought. How could these people she knew, her own family, be involved in kidnapping and baby selling?

"Well, it's Rayburn's operation, at least here in Moss Creek, but I've managed to make myself important to him over the years by supplying vehicles and buildings."

"You've been using my father's company to assist a human-trafficking ring."

"And making myself a lot of money doing it." He grinned, seemingly pleased with himself.

A car door slammed outside and David leapt to his feet.

Janice ran to the window. "It's Collin!"

Rebecca's heart lurched with hope until David pulled out a gun. "I'll take care of him."

"Don't hurt him!" she cried. All the anger she'd felt toward him evaporated the moment she saw the gun and knew his life was in danger. "He doesn't know anything. Janice knocked me out before I could call him."

He glanced at Janice. "It's true. She never had the chance to call him. He's probably just here hoping to make up with her."

David slipped the gun into his pocket. "Then I'll get rid of him another way." He looked at Janice as the knock came at the front door. He grabbed the duct tape from the table, ripped off a piece and clamped it over Rebecca's mouth. "I will shoot him if I have to. Don't make a sound or try to cry out for his attention and he'll walk away from here alive. Do you understand me?"

She nodded, willing to remain quiet to keep David from hurting Collin. How had she never seen the coldness in David before today? He'd hidden it well.

The knock came again and David hurried to the door. He opened it and Rebecca heard him greeting Collin cordially, as if he wasn't holding her captive only a few feet away. The man was a monster who'd been living right in front of her for years.

Rebecca craned her neck, trying to see Collin. She'd been a fool to leave him. She'd walked away from him and right into the lion's den. Had it been their plan all along to get her away from Collin? Was her own cousin and her husband behind the threatening notes and attacks on her life? Had Janice told her about Collin just to separate her from him?

Part of her wanted to try to scream to get Collin's attention but David had promised to kill him if she did and something in his eyes told her he wouldn't hesitate. But if she didn't try to cry out, would Collin even know she was in trouble? Would he even bother trying to find her?

"I want to apologize to her," Collin was saying. "How can I say I'm sorry if she won't see me?"

"Give her some time," David told him, his voice full of feigned empathy. "Maybe in a few days, she'll feel more like talking."

A few days? Where would she be in a few days? Would she even still be alive? If she was, knowing the kind of operation Rayburn was running, she would probably wish she was dead.

As David closed the door, tears sprang to Rebecca's eyes. Collin was gone and he had no idea how much she needed him. She'd wasted her opportunity with him by letting something that happened years ago send her running from him. The money didn't matter and neither did their past mistakes. Because now she knew she would give anything to have another chance to tell him how much she loved him.

"That was ugly," David said, coming back into the room and kneeling beside Rebecca. "He must really love you. It's a shame. I suppose now, finally, he'll be able to move on." He stood and pulled out his phone and dialed a number. "Jack, it's David. We have a problem. Rebecca knows about Matthew." He listened, then nodded and ended the call.

"What did he say?" Janice asked him. "Does he want us to kill her?"

Rebecca sucked in a breath and waited to hear her fate.

"No. Call the nanny and see if she can watch Matthew. I'm going to load Rebecca into the back of the SUV. Rayburn wants us to bring her to him. He said he was looking forward to taking care of her personally." He smiled when he said it and glanced Rebecca's way.

Fear shuddered through her. Rayburn had already tried to have her killed multiple times. With David and Janice delivering her to him like a turkey trussed up for Thanksgiving, he was sure to succeed this time.

He pulled a syringe from his pocket and Rebecca flinched.

"Don't worry," he assured her. "It's just a sedative we keep on hand to deal with the unruly types." He kneeled down and pressed the needle into her neck and after only a few moments, she felt its effects. The room began to spin and David and Janice's conversation sounded far away. She was losing consciousness quickly and although she knew this wouldn't kill her, what was waiting for her when she awoke would.

She was going to die today.

He probably deserved the communication blackout he was getting from Rebecca, but that didn't mean he liked it. He couldn't keep her safe if she wouldn't even return his phone calls or come to the door to talk. And he wasn't giving up on her, not until he knew the threat to her life was over.

David had been insistent at the door that she didn't want to see him. He knew she was angry, but she had to see reason soon and at least be civil enough to allow him to keep her safe. She couldn't have had time to hire a bodyguard yet and, if she had, he would have come to the door to insist Collin leave. He turned and looked back at the house, hoping to catch a glimpse of Rebecca peering out at him as he left. He wanted so badly to see her face, even if only for a moment, to know she was okay, but he spotted no curtains moving anywhere.

It felt wrong to leave but what else was he going to do? Storm inside and demand she talk to him? She'd made it crystal clear she didn't want to see him. It was time he accepted it and moved on.

But he couldn't. He just couldn't. He'd made a vow to himself to protect her and he would see it through. He owed her at least that.

He got into his car, started the engine and drove away. She had court scheduled for this afternoon. It was the one thing he knew she wouldn't miss, so he would be there, too, just to make sure she was safe and hopefully convince her to talk to him.

Rebecca awoke on a hard surface. She opened her eyes and realized she was lying on concrete. She was still bound, but the duct tape had been replaced with zip ties. She tried to sit up but her head swam and she lay down again. Someone called her name and Rebecca jerked fully awake.

Janice sat on a step a few feet away watching her.

"Why couldn't you just leave well enough alone? David and I tried to stop you from digging into this. The notes, the warning on your wall, even my getting attacked were all meant to keep you from investigating further. Rayburn wanted you dead but we thought we could make him see reason if you would stop, but you didn't. You refused to stop even for me. Even when I was in danger."

The guilt she'd felt at seeing her cousin's bruises faded now that she knew the truth. "You were never in danger, were you? It was all for show."

"Yes, it was a show for you, but I guess keeping me safe wasn't as important as protecting some girl who isn't even family."

Missy! She was talking about Missy. Janice might know where they'd taken her. It was possible she was even here in the same building where they'd brought Rebecca. "You know where she is, don't you?"

Janice sneered. "Your precious girl is gone,

Rebecca. Because of you and your meddling, Jack had to ship her off to another provider."

"Another provider?" Rebecca gasped at the implication. "You mean another kidnapper, don't you?"

"You cost us money, and Jack isn't going to let you get away with that. Besides, you've become a liability to me, as well. As long as you're alive, Matthew is in danger from you."

"I would never hurt Matthew."

"No, but you would keep on and on until you finally shut down our operation and that would cost me my son. I'm sorry, Rebecca, but I can't allow that."

Rebecca could understand her cousin's desire for a child, but she also knew the pain of losing a baby and Janice's knowingly taking another woman's baby was unfathomable. If she was capable of that, what else was her cousin capable of?

"You have to know this is wrong, Jan."

"What's wrong is that some teenage girl with no job and no money can have a child and I can't. Life isn't fair, Rebecca. We're just leveling the playing field."

Rebecca saw there was no getting through to her. She'd justified her actions and those actions had led her down a dark path.

Janice stood and walked out. Tears slipped

down Rebecca's face. How had such evil existed right under her nose and she'd never had a clue? She'd considered Janice like a sister to her for most of their lives. How was it possible her cousin was responsible for the disappearance of teens under her care? Rebecca had spent her life caring for others, while Janice had spent her life using them to get whatever she wanted.

God, how has everything gone so wrong?

She'd tried to stay strong after her life fell apart. She'd lost her baby, her husband and her future all in one fell swoop, but she'd always tried to remain strong and believe God was in control. But how much more could she take? She'd tried to live her life to mean something, tried to make a difference. But now, just when it seemed things were turning around for her and Collin, her life had spiraled and she was going to lose it all again.

Janice was right. Life wasn't fair.

Collin arrived at the courthouse an hour before court was to begin. He didn't see Rebecca so he asked the bailiff to give her a message that he was here and would like to speak with her.

"She hasn't arrived yet," the man stated, "but I'll tell her when she does."

An hour later, court still hadn't begun and Collin approached the bailiff again.

"Rebecca hasn't arrived and no one has been able to reach her. We may have to re-schedule all these cases if she doesn't show up."

Something was wrong. Collin knew it the moment he heard Rebecca hadn't shown up. She wouldn't leave these cases in limbo with-out a good reason. She'd fought him and even put her own safety at risk to prepare for this day. She wouldn't just not show up.

Collin phoned Kent and updated him on what was happening. "I think something is very wrong," he said. "Rebecca is missing."

Kent phoned the courthouse then called him back. "They've been trying to reach her all afternoon. I tried, too, and her phone is going straight to voice mail."

"She's been staying at her cousin's house. I was there this morning and David assured me she was there, but she didn't want to see me."

"I'll meet you there in ten minutes," Kent told him. "She'll either let me in or I'll get a warrant."

Collin ended the call and headed for his car and back to Janice's. Recalling how she'd fought him about coming to court today, he knew Rebecca would have been there if she'd been able. Something as minor as a fight between them wouldn't have kept her away.

Something was very wrong.

God, please let her be okay.

Fear gripped him. He was afraid something had happened to Rebecca and he'd been unable to prevent it. Perhaps something had happened to the whole family. Had someone broken in after he'd left and disposed of David, Janice and the baby as well? The thought sickened him.

Collin was at the house before Kent, but he arrived only minutes later. He was anxious about barging inside, but he felt in his gut that something was wrong. Rebecca would not have missed court. Very few things could have prevented her from coming and he shuddered to think what those might be.

Kent marched up to the house and knocked. Collin heard sounds from inside and a moment later, the door opened. It wasn't Janice who answered but a woman Collin didn't recognize.

Kent pulled out his badge. "I'm Investigator Morris. I need to see Rebecca Mason."

The woman looked confused. "I haven't seen Rebecca."

"Who are you?" Collin asked.

"My name is Lily. I'm the nanny."

"What about Janice or David? Are they home?"

"No, they're gone, too. Today was supposed to be my day off, but Janice called a while ago and asked me if I could watch Matthew. She and David had to go out of town for a few days."

"Did they say where they were going?" Collin asked.

"I didn't ask. It's not unusual for them to take an impromptu vacation."

Kent glanced at Collin. "How likely is it that Janice would take a vacation while her cousin is in danger?"

"Not very. They're cousins but they were raised more like sisters. Besides, where is Rebecca? Did Janice or David tell you where she went?"

"Only that she left town. When I asked about the attacks against her, Janice told me she left town to get away from the danger. It made sense to me so I didn't question it." In the house, the baby began to fuss. "I really need to get back to Matthew."

Collin glanced upstairs. "Mind if I look at the room where she was staying?"

The nanny shook her head and Collin raced

up the stairs. As he did, he heard Kent telling the nanny that he needed contact information for the Millers.

He opened the door to the room where Rebecca had been staying. Her suitcase was on a bench by the window and her clothes were still inside. Her briefcase with her court papers sat on the chair by the window. No way she would leave town while these kids' lives hung in the balance. No matter how frightened or angry she was at him, she wouldn't have just left without at least tying that up. In the adjoining bathroom, he saw her makeup bag on the cabinet along with the chain and ring she wore. He picked up the ring and fingered it. He might believe she'd leave this behind after how angry she'd been at him over his taking money from her father before he left her, but it wasn't likely she would leave without her clothes, her purse, or her makeup.

That stinging in his gut came again. This was wrong. This was so wrong. It was more than a communication blackout. She wasn't petty enough to put herself in danger or risk the lives of the foster kids she helped. She was gone.

He slipped the necklace into his pocket and went back downstairs. "All of Rebecca's things are still here." He turned to the nanny. "When you saw her last, did she mention anything about leaving town?"

Lily shook her head. "No. In fact, she said she was looking forward to spending time with Matthew. She loves this little boy."

"What about David and Janice? You said you saw them today?"

"Yes, just a few hours ago."

"Both of them?"

"Yes, they were both here when I arrived. David was loading the car. They apologized for the short notice and even offered to pay me double for keeping Matthew."

"What were they driving?"

"Janice's SUV. David's car is still in the garage."

"Have you tried to call them?"

Kent nodded. "I just tried. No answer. I also had Lily try to call from her phone. I thought they might answer if they thought it was about their child." He turned to Lily and handed her his card. "Let me know if they call or return home or if you hear anything else about Rebecca. It's important that we find her."

They walked out and Lily closed and locked the door behind them.

A terrible thought struck Collin and he glanced back at the house, spotting Lily with baby Matthew through the open curtain.

Kent obviously saw his concerned expression. "What is it?"

"I've seen terrible things while I was overseas. Things that still make me shudder when I think about them. There is evil in this world, Kent."

"You think David and Janice are involved in this?"

"Rebecca is trying to expose a baby-selling ring, and her cousin and her husband just adopted a child a year ago. Now, they've all disappeared. That's too coincidental for my taste."

Kent nodded and pulled out his phone. "I'll have their phones tracked. If they're turned on, we'll find them."

Collin nodded. "I'm heading over to Rebecca's dad's house. I want to know everything he knows about Matthew's adoption."

Collin climbed into his car and started the engine. As Kent sped away in his car, the gravity of what was happening hit him. Rebecca was in danger and it was his fault. He'd promised to keep her safe and, once again, he'd failed her.

He may have blown his second chance at

forever with her, but he would find her and bring her home safely if it was the last thing he ever did.

Rebecca stiffened and pulled away when the door swung open and Dr. Jack Rayburn stepped inside. She wished she could get free and scratch his eyes out. This was pure evil standing before her—a man who traded women and children like products instead of living beings, a man who had sent people to try to kill her.

He stepped into the room, David and Janice following behind him. "Well, well, well. Rebecca Mason, you've caused me and my operation a lot of trouble."

"Good." She was glad he'd suffered even if it was only monetarily. "Tell me this. Why kidnap these women? Why not just wait until the babies are born and snatch them then?"

He shook his head. "People notice missing babies more than they notice missing girls. We will snatch a child if necessary, if we need to fill a specific request, but ultimately, this is simpler and creates less police presence. After all, who cares about a bunch of missing teenaged girls?"

She pulled at her restraints, seething at the

emotionless manner in which he spoke. "I do," she told him.

"I know you do, Rebecca. I've seen how much you care and it's unfortunate. It's the reason you're here. It's the reason I had to send my best asset, Joanne Pierson, away and send my men, Jimmy and Devo, after you. Now, their faces are all over the police's radar. I had someone in the sheriff's office helping me with things like that, but thanks to you and your friends, he's been exposed and is on the run. We'll have to relocate, too, but that's okay. We'll start over again in a new place. You see, you can't stop us, Rebecca. You've been chasing after something that's too big for you to stop."

She looked at Janice, trying one last time. "Please don't let him do this to me."

"You were trying to take my baby." Janice started to come at her, but David held her back.

"He doesn't belong to you."

David pushed his wife away as she lunged for Rebecca again. "Matthew is our child," he told Rebecca. "You had no right to imply otherwise."

She motioned at Dr. Rayburn. "If you're doing business with him, then you're wrong. He steals children from their mothers."

Dr. Rayburn kneeled beside her, his eyes still cold and unfeeling. "I provide a valuable service that you can't possibly understand. I'm not the only one, either. I'm only one spoke in a wheel operating all across the country."

Janice had hinted at the same thing. That meant Missy could be anywhere by now if she wasn't already dead. "What are you going to do to me?"

He reached for her cheek and stroked it, an act that caused her stomach to curdle. "You, my dear, could be useful. You're still young enough to bear children for us." He sighed. "But I suspect you'll be more trouble than you're worth. Still, I'll leave your future up to my business associates. Once you're locked away on the other side of the country, you might not be so stubborn. But you'll be someone else's problem then. Not mine."

An image of her future flashed through her mind. Beaten, raped, forced to give birth, then have her child stolen from her. She would end up like Missy. But she had one thing Missy didn't have. She had Collin to look out for her.

Except that she didn't.

She'd pushed him away. Now, he would forever believe she'd hated him. Would he even try to contact her again after the way she'd treated him? She wouldn't blame him if he didn't, but she needed him now. She needed Collin to find her. He was her only hope now.

No, that wasn't true. She had God on her side and He certainly knew she was in trouble. But one question entered her mind. Would He help her now after the way she'd turned her back? She knew He would. She was counting on it.

"Now to the other matter," Rayburn said, turning to the couple behind him. He focused in on Janice. "You've compromised my operation and I can't allow that." He pulled a gun from his pocket and fired. The look of surprise on Janice's face as she realized she'd been shot faded a moment later when she collapsed. David caught her and lowered her to the floor.

"Why did you do that?" he cried.

"Because she was a loose cannon."

David looked at him. "She was my wife!"

"Tomorrow morning, you'll report her missing to the police. By the afternoon, her body will be found in an empty motel room along with a note explaining that she took her own life because she discovered you were having an affair."

"What? No. I wouldn't do that. I love my wife and son."

"You'll explain that she's been dealing with depression and had neglected the baby. It was your intention to take custody of the child."

He lowered his head and shook it in despair but even Rebecca could see he would do as instructed. "How am I going to let my son believe that his mother killed herself?"

"You won't have to worry about that, David. I'm taking the child."

"No, you're not."

Rebecca gasped at the mention of Matthew and the thought of Rayburn touching him.

"Your wife has opened a can of worms for me. I have to pull up stakes here and that will cost me a lot of money. The boy is still young enough to fetch me a good profit. When they find your wife, they'll also find a note saying she's killed him and hidden his body. It won't be found and soon enough the police will assume he's dead, too. You'll be devastated but you'll move on." He gave David a hard stare. "Can you do that, David?" He lifted his gun again. "Or do I need to make this a murder-suicide?"

Rebecca found herself rooting for David, hoping he would rise up against this madman and end this insanity. She could see he truly loved Janice and he was about to lose his son as well. But, after a moment of staring at the weapon, David shook his head. "No, I can do it."

Rebecca couldn't believe Janice was gone, but her cousin wasn't moving. And now Matthew was going to be sold. Hot tears flooded her face as guilt moved through her. If she hadn't pushed, if she hadn't insisted... She shoved aside those thoughts. No, this was not her fault, no matter how David's eyes seemed to blame her. He was the one who'd brought Rayburn into their lives. And Rayburn was the one who'd killed Janice.

Collin found Rebecca's father in his office at the house.

"Have you heard from Rebecca?"

"Not since our blowup yesterday. She's staying with David and Janice."

"She's not there. Her clothes and stuff are still in the guest room, but she's gone. Plus, she missed court this afternoon. Are you sure you haven't talked to her?"

"I haven't." He picked up his phone. "I'll call David."

"Please try. Kent and I went to the house. The nanny was there and she said that David and Janice had gone out of town. We all tried calling and they didn't answer."

Bob placed a call then shook his head. "It's going straight to voice mail."

"Something has happened to Rebecca. She wouldn't have not shown up to court today. Her job is too important to her. She takes her responsibility to those kids she mentors seriously."

"And David and Janice? Do you think something has happened to them, too?"

"No, Bob, I think they're involved in whatever has happened to Rebecca."

He shook his head. "No, I've raised Janice since she was a child. David practically runs my company. They would never be involved in anything like this."

"What do you know about Matthew's adoption?"

"What do you mean?"

"Where did they get him? Did they use an adoption agency? Do you know the lawyer who processed the adoption?"

"I—I don't know. He was a friend of David's from school. I didn't delve into their business. I was just thankful they were finally able to have a child. They'd tried for so long."

Collin shook his head. He didn't like it. "You said David practically runs the company now. He would have access to all the company information. He would know which buildings were being used and which were sitting empty."

Bob saw where he was going with this line of thinking. "You think he provided the building where that girl was held?"

"It makes sense, doesn't it? Rebecca suspected someone at Mason Industries was involved. Aside from you, who knows more about the business?"

He shook his head, clearly still refusing to believe this. "This can't be right."

Collin's phone rang and he saw it was Kent calling. "Please tell me you have some good news."

"Not yet. Rebecca's cell phone is state-issued for her job so we were able to access her records quickly. Unfortunately, it's not pinging anywhere. It's probably off, but we'll be watching if it turns back on."

"What about David's or Janice's?"

"It'll be harder to get a warrant for their cell phones, but I've issued a BOLO for Janice's SUV and am monitoring their credit cards. We'll find them."

Collin wondered if it would be in time. "What's happening with your Deputy Seaver? Has he given you any information? Can we use him to find Rebecca?"

"No, we haven't been able to locate him. He cleaned out his bank accounts and skipped town."

As they ended the call, Collin felt like screaming in frustration and anger. How had he let this happen? David and Janice had taken Rebecca and they'd been right under his nose the entire time.

Logic began to seep through his anger and he tried to think rationally. David and Janice were the all-American couple but it seemed unlikely they were behind a trafficking ring that abducted women and sold children on the black market. They didn't have the connections to build an operation like that. But Jack Rayburn did and Collin was banking on him not only being involved, but also deeply invested in the operation.

"I have to go," he told Bob.

"Where are you going?"

"Following up on the only lead I have—Dr. Rayburn. If I can find him, he'll eventually lead me to Rebecca."

He knew it was a long shot, but it was the only one he had left.

Rebecca had no idea how long she'd been locked up but it seemed like days. She was exhausted and stiff from sitting in one position and she was thirsty and weak with hunger. She'd spent hours rubbing the hard plastic zip tie against a sharp piece of metal piping she was bound to with no success. But it was the only thing she could do—that and pray.

And she hadn't stopped praying. This couldn't be the end for her. This couldn't be the end for her and Collin. And the bad guys could not be allowed to win.

She pressed the zip tie against the metal and continued to rub for as long as she could then fell against the wall, exhausted.

Collin, where are you?

TEN

Collin drove to Jackson and staked out the doctor's office. If anyone could lead him to Rebecca, it would be Rayburn. He phoned the office and checked with the receptionist to confirm Rayburn was seeing patients. He parked and waited, his mind circling around all the evidence. Rayburn was the key to it all. He was the one who could find the girls, teenage girls with pregnancies. As a doctor, he would also have access to their background and would know they were in foster care. Few people would miss a pregnant runaway foster child. They would be the invisible victims in Rayburn's sick scheme.

But the problem with a stakeout was that it gave him time to think, time to mull over the past several days and all that had transpired. He'd gotten Rebecca back, his Rebecca, only to lose her again. He'd been foolish enough to believe that he could make up for how he'd failed her, but now he'd failed her all over again.

It was a vicious circle.

He thought he'd long ago given up the need to control everything, to shoulder the blame, but this time he was to blame…wasn't he? Everything that had happened had happened because of that horrible decision he'd made twelve years ago. It wasn't fair that Rebecca was still paying the price for his sins.

His phone rang and he answered it. Kent had news. "Lily the nanny called me. She spoke to David and told him we were looking for them."

"You talked to him?"

"No. By the time I reached the house, he'd already picked up the baby and left again. They're gone, Collin. Now that they know we're on to them, they'll have to disappear."

And now baby Matthew was caught up in whatever was going on, too. Rebecca would hate that more than anything.

"Call me if you hear anything else."

Rebecca had no idea how long she'd been trapped in this room. Hours? Days? But she knew her time was limited. She was so tired and weak from hunger, but she couldn't give up. If she did, her life—whether Rayburn

killed her or sold her into the baby business—
was over. She had to keep trying to escape.

She rubbed the zip ties against the metal
again. It was a slow process and her wrists
were more frayed than her binds, but she had
to keep going. Escape was her only option.

Tears slipped from her eyes but she didn't
even know if they were from frustration or
fear or for what she'd be losing if she didn't
break free. She stopped sawing and hung her
head.

She hated feeling so helpless and alone.
She'd been alone for years, afraid to take another chance with anyone. Afraid to confide
in anyone, even God, for fear of being hurt
again in the way she'd been with Collin. But
the past week, reconnecting with Collin, had
reminded her of what living really felt like.
She'd wasted so much of her life protecting
her heart. Now, all she wanted was to risk
it. To give Collin a second chance and to be
happy.

Now, she'd probably lost that chance.

She would disappear and Collin would be
the one left alone and abandoned, believing
that she hadn't loved him, that she'd never forgiven him. It wasn't the future she wanted for
him. She wanted to tell him the truth—that
she'd never stopped loving him and that she

did forgive him. It didn't matter anymore that he'd taken money from her father. He'd said he'd felt like a failure for not being a good provider, and she believed him now that it had been for the hospital bills. She was such a fool for pushing him away.

She may never get the chance to tell Collin those things, but she could tell God. She'd kept Him at a distance for years, protecting herself even from her faith for fear of being overwhelmed by her emotions. She'd allowed bitterness and resentment to wiggle their way into her soul and she'd lost out on so much life because of it.

"I'm so sorry," she cried. "Please forgive me."

She leaned up against the pipe she was tied to and sobbed. She'd finally pushed through her pain and anger, but it was too late to make a difference in her life.

He was good at being invisible when needed. He'd learned it during his army training and had used it on many missions during his time with the rangers and as a covert operative for the CIA. Tonight, he needed to be invisible as he followed Dr. Rayburn from his office. The doctor drove across town and Collin followed behind, careful to remain back far enough to not be spotted but close enough that he wouldn't lose him.

The doctor drove for nearly an hour before he turned into a long drive that took him to a warehouse, but not one that had been on the list Rebecca's father had given them. It made sense. David was involved in the business enough to keep a property off Bob's radar and off the official reports. The lights in the parking lot were off but there were lights inside and Collin spotted not only the doctor's vehicle, but also two white vans parked by the door where he'd entered, the same kind of vans used to abduct Missy from the motel.

Collin took out his gun and checked it. Anyone who drove out to an abandoned warehouse in the middle of the night had to have something to hide and he was guessing it had something to do with Rebecca's disappearance. Whatever it was, Collin was going to find out.

He got out of his car and approached the building, noting the Mason Industries stenciled on the outside. He scanned the area and spotted security cameras. He wasn't getting inside unnoticed. That didn't matter. Logic told him he should go back to his car and phone the police. He shouldn't be going in alone with no backup, but his gut told him there was no time to bring the police in. Besides, what was he going to tell them to motivate them to come? That he'd followed Rayburn to an abandoned factory but hadn't yet discovered anything illegal happening? No, he couldn't wait and he doubted they would come, anyway, and Kent was too far to make it there in time. Collin was going inside and he wasn't coming out until he had Rebecca with him.

He moved closer to the two white vans and peeked through the window of one, seeing no one inside. When he looked in the other however, he spotted something in the back beneath a sheet. It looked like a body. His gut clenched as he noticed how small it was. Too small to be a grown man, but the figure was just right for a woman's body. He opened the door and climbed inside. He had to look. He had to know if this body was Rebecca. He lifted the sheet and felt only a momentary relief that it wasn't her before it registered that the body was Janice.

Now was the time to call in the police. A dead body gave them plenty of reasons to come. He reached into his pocket for his phone, but it wasn't there. He must have left it in his car. He stared at the body and debated for only a moment before deciding not to go back for it. If they'd killed Janice, what had they done with Rebecca? The urgency of the situation skyrocketed. He had to find her before she ended up lying beside her cousin in the back of the van.

Once her tears were spent, Rebecca sat up and began sawing at her binds again. It was all she could do aside from giving up and she wasn't ready for that yet.

She felt the hard plastic start to give and her heart lurched. She rubbed harder and noticed a spot on the bottom wearing thin. She concentrated on that area and when it gave, she quickly slipped off the zip tie and tumbled backward. She was free! Her wrists were raw and bleeding, but she was free from those restraints. Now, to get out of this room and escape from this building.

A newfound determination filled her. Missy had escaped these people and so could she, but thoughts of Missy reminded her that she wasn't the only one being held captive in this building. And Rayburn was making plans to leave town tonight. If she escaped on her own, these girls might disappear again, this time never to be found. She couldn't leave without them even if it decreased their chances of escaping.

But first she had to find a way out of this room.

She moved toward the door and pressed her ear against it, listening. She heard nothing outside the door. She hadn't noticed anyone standing guard when the others had come and gone. She pulled at the handle and found it unlocked. Yes! Apparently, they didn't feel the need to lock her in since she'd been bound.

She opened the door and peeked into the hallway. The corridor was clear. She slipped out. She wasn't familiar with this building and had no idea where the girls were being held or where the exits were, but she would find them, hopefully before anyone realized she was missing.

She stopped when she heard noises and slipped into a nook to hide. A door opened and a big man with a gun exited the room. Behind him, she saw a group of women huddled together, fear flashing in their eyes. The girls! They were being gathered together to leave. As he closed the door, he slipped a padlock on it then disappeared down the hallway.

Rebecca waited for him to leave then rushed toward the door. She pulled at the lock. It was locked in place and wouldn't budge.

Without the key, she couldn't get inside and set those women free. And she wasn't leaving without them. She wished for a hairpin but she wasn't sure she could pick the lock even if she had one. She glanced around and saw a crowbar on the floor. If she could jam it into the lock, maybe it would break. She grabbed it and jammed it into the lock but it didn't budge. She tried again. Still nothing.

Tears rolled down her cheeks. She couldn't break it, but she couldn't leave without these girls, either.

She was in a no-win situation.

Collin entered the factory, gun raised and ready for anything. He wasn't leaving until he found Rebecca. He was ready to take on whoever got in his way. He spotted a camera, pulled out his knife and quickly clipped the wires leading to it. He repeated that with each one he saw as he moved through the building. Movement from a long hall grabbed his attention. He raised his gun and spun into the door. "Don't move."

He stopped when he saw big brown eyes full of fear staring back at him. She was holding a crowbar and ready to use it as a weapon.

His heart jumped. She was alive!

"Rebecca!"

She ran to him and fell into his arms. "Collin! I thought I would never see you again."

"I'm here." His heart soared with gratitude. *Thank You, Lord, for letting me find her safe.* He soaked in the feeling of her in his arms then pulled away, noting the new bruising on her face and the sores on her wrists. They weren't out of the woods yet. She wouldn't truly be safe until they were away from this place. "Let's get you out of here."

"No, not yet. I can't leave. This door… There are women behind this door. We can't leave without them."

Although she was his primary concern and all his heart wanted to do was run with her, he checked that emotion. She was right. They couldn't leave the others behind. He quickly snipped the wires of the camera he spotted above the door. If anyone was watching, they would have already seen her and be on the way, but he had to risk it. He grabbed the crowbar from her hands.

"I tried to break it but I couldn't."

She didn't have the muscle it took. He jammed the crowbar into the lock and put his weight behind it. It took a few moments but the lock split. He slipped it off, grabbed his gun and swung open the door. The women inside squealed with fear until Rebecca hurried past him and rushed inside to reassure them.

"We're only here to help. We're not going to hurt you. We have to get you all out of here. Now, we need to leave quickly and quietly before someone sees us. Is there anyone else in the building?"

"Yes," one girl said. "A baby. I saw them bring him inside and set up a crib down the hall when they were taking me to be examined."

"That has to be Matthew," Collin said. "Lily called and told us David came by and picked him up once he heard we were looking for him."

"We have to find him," Rebecca said. "I won't leave without him."

Collin nodded and ushered the women out the door. "Head down the hall and turn to the right. I've cut the camera wires so they can't see you. Go out the door and get into one of the white vans but be quiet. We'll be out once we find the boy."

The girls moved quickly and quietly down the hallway as Collin and Rebecca checked the other doors. Finally, she opened one and saw a playpen. Matthew squealed with delight at seeing her and stood up in the bed.

"Hi there, sweetheart." She scooped him up in her arms.

"Let's go," Collin said, thankful they'd found the child, but anxious to get out before they were discovered.

Running with a one-year-old would not be easy and Collin prayed Matthew wouldn't make any noises that might alert David or the others. It didn't matter. They weren't leaving him here with those monsters.

They hurried down the hall and found the door but as they reached it, Collin heard someone call out that she was gone.

They'd been found out!

Doors opened and Collin spotted Rayburn head out of the office, followed by David.

"Run!" he told Rebecca. He raised his gun and fired, causing Rayburn and the rest of them to duck for cover.

"Get them!" Rayburn called out.

He spun around and saw Rebecca already through the door and hopping into the back of the van along with the other girls. He headed for the van. It was their only hope for escaping now. The girls slammed the back doors shut as he hopped into the driver's seat, reached under the steering wheel and had the van hot-wired in a matter of seconds. Rebecca was urging him on the entire time as the girls huddled in the back. Finally, the engine kicked on and Collin pushed the van into gear and took off. He spotted a group of people, including Rayburn, hurrying from the warehouse as they roared away. Two men started shooting and the girls began to scream and cry.

"Everyone get down," Collin shouted as he floored the accelerator and sped away. In the side mirrors he spotted men climbing into the other van and pursuing them. They had to get to a main road and get help before those guys caught up to them. "Rebecca, take the wheel." When she slid over and grabbed the steering wheel, he shimmied to the passenger's seat and pulled out his gun. He leaned out the window and fired several shots at the van pursuing them. The van avoided them all. They returned fire and Rebecca swerved, nearly throwing him from the van. He gripped the window and slid back inside. He expected her to be frantic, but she looked calm and composed as she drove. She was strong. She had always been strong in the face of adversity. It was one of the things he'd always loved about her...one of the things he still loved about her.

"I'm out of ammunition," he told her.

She glanced at the mirror. "They're gaining on us. What should we do?"

He wished for a cell phone to call for help

but there was none coming. They were on their own until they could get closer to town.

He saw her eyes widen and she tensed. "They're coming."

The van swerved around them and sped up, pulling along beside them. It jerked, forcing Rebecca off the road. The girls screamed in the back and Matthew began to cry as the van left the asphalt and slammed into a tree. Collin was thrown forward, slamming his head against the dash. The world seemed to turn upside down as he glanced over at Rebecca and saw her slumped against the steering wheel, unconscious. He was helpless to do anything for her as darkness enveloped him and all he could do was plead for God to help them.

Rebecca's ears were ringing as she opened her eyes. They were still in the van but it was quiet now except for the sound in the distance of footsteps approaching and the baby's cries. Beside her, Collin was unconscious. She looked in the back. Most of the girls were beginning to stir after the accident. She unbuckled and leaned over Collin. Blood was oozing from a gash on his forehead where he'd hit his head. She shook him, trying to awaken him, but he didn't move.

"Is everyone okay?" she asked and the girls began to moan and move around.

One of them looked out the window. "They're coming."

Rebecca glanced out and saw two men with guns approaching. Jimmy and Devo. The girls backed up as if that would prevent them from being recaptured. "We have to get out of here." She turned back to Collin and looked for his gun, scooping it up and checking it. It was empty.

"Come out now," a voice commanded from outside, then the back doors swung open and the girls were pulled from the van. Someone else opened Rebecca's door and a big hand grabbed her and pulled her out, yanking her back to the road, where Rayburn was waiting.

He flashed her a smug grin as his goons dragged her to him.

"Let me go!" she demanded.

Rayburn signaled and the girls were herded into the back of the other van.

"You've caused me a great deal of trouble, Miss Mason, and now you've cost me a van as well."

One of the goons came up to him. "There's a guy in the van. He's knocked out from the crash."

Rayburn looked at Rebecca then smiled

again. He turned back to the man and gave an order. "Shoot him."

"Will do, boss."

Rebecca struggled against the grip on her arm as the man walked back down the incline and toward the van. He moved to the passenger's side, out of their sight, but a moment later, a gunshot sent her stomach plummeting. He'd just shot Collin while he was helpless and unconscious.

"What kind of a man are you?" she cried to Rayburn. "Shooting a man when he's unconscious. That's low even for you."

"He was in my way, Rebecca. That's what I do to people who get in my way. Unfortunately, you'll learn that lesson as well."

Hot tears threatened her but she pushed them back. She would not cry, not now. She wouldn't let Rayburn know how he'd just devastated her by shooting Collin. Besides, she had to remain calm if she and the girls had any hope of escaping again. They had to make their move while they were out in the open.

Rayburn dragged her toward his car, opened the back door and shoved her inside. Now was her chance. She pushed the door back at him as he tried to close it, forcing him backward with all the strength she possessed. He lost his balance and stumbled, giving her the opportunity to dash away from the car. She ran to the back of the van as Rayburn shouted out for Devo to go after her. She made it to the back and managed to tackle the man before he was aware of what was happening.

The girls gasped as someone grabbed her from behind and pressed a knife to her throat that ended her struggling. "Don't do that again," Rayburn sneered.

This was it. She was going to die. He would slit her throat and toss her on the side of the road and these girls who needed her help would vanish for good, his criminal enterprise continuing on with only a bump in the road.

Devo pushed to his feet, groaning. Rayburn turned to him. "Get up, you fool. And go find out what's taking Jimmy so long. He should have come back by now."

"Jimmy's dead," a voice from behind them said and Rebecca's heart leaped with joy at the sound.

Rayburn spun around, keeping the knife pressed against her neck. Behind the van doors stood Collin, alive and aiming a gun at Rayburn.

"Collin!"

"Recognize this?" Collin asked him, waggling the gun he was holding. "I took it off your guy right before I shot him."

Rayburn dug the knife into her skin to make his point. "I'll slit her throat right now if you don't drop that gun."

Collin didn't flinch. "You do and you'll be dead before she hits the ground. Let her go and you get to live."

Devo came around the van and Collin fired, sending him to the ground before turning the gun back on Rayburn. "That's both of your men down, Rayburn. You're next."

Something about Collin's assured manner gave her hope. He'd been in situations like this before and knew how to handle them. Whatever he did, he couldn't give up the gun or they were both dead. She knew it and she was certain Collin knew it as well.

Blood was smeared on his face but he didn't seem to let it bother him. His stance was firm and his eyes fixed and ready. By contrast, she felt Rayburn tense and his heartbeat increase. He was caged in and like a wild animal, he would fight when cornered.

This was not going to end well.

God, help us!

She didn't even know the words to pray. Collin had a decision to make and if it meant sacrificing herself to save those girls and end this operation once and for all, she was willing to make it. She just wasn't sure Collin was willing to let her. He would fight until the end.

The air stood still around her. She saw Collin fire and felt the knife dig into her throat. She couldn't even cry out as pain overwhelmed her. Her knees buckled and she fell forward, tumbling to the ground. She touched her neck and felt something warm and wet. Blood. She watched Rayburn fall and heard the screams of the girls in the van, but it was all background noise to the sound of Collin's scream as he ran to her and hovered over her.

"Hang on," he told her as he pulled off his jacket and pressed it to her.

She knew the truth. They were out in the middle of nowhere with no cell phone and no one on the way to help them. And she saw the truth of her injury on Collin's face. She was going to bleed out right here on the side of the road.

He shouted something to the girls, who were now hovering over her also. But when he turned back to her there was fear glowing in his green eyes, fear of losing her. She wanted to tell him it was going to be okay. That she was okay with the Lord now, but mostly she wanted to tell him how much she loved him and had always loved him.

He shook his head. "Don't try to talk, Rebecca. We're getting help."

She reached up and touched his cheek, her own hand covered in blood. "I love you," she whispered to him, pushing past the pain and effort of speaking.

His face was the last thing she saw as darkness formed around him and his words were the last thing she heard. "I love you, too, my Rebecca."

Rebecca awoke to the sound of monitors beeping. She opened her eyes and saw she was in a hospital room. Her neck hurt and she felt weak. She turned her head and spotted Collin asleep in the recliner by her bed. She reached out to him, touching his hand and he squirmed, then jolted awake.

"Rebecca, you're awake."

"What happened?" she asked. It came out only as a whisper and cut her throat.

"Rayburn attacked you. Don't you remember?"

Images began to return of him pressing the knife to her throat and Collin shooting him. "The girls. What happened to the girls and Matthew?"

"They're fine. The girls are being questioned by the FBI about the people that were holding them. It seems Rayburn wasn't lying about being a part of a greater organization. Most of those girls were taken from other states and brought here. David is cooperating with the FBI in the hopes of getting a lighter sentence. He's given them names and locations of other organizations. The lead agent told me they're already planning raids of three different operations across two states."

"What about Matthew?"

"He's fine. I phoned your father. He came by and picked him up."

"Missy. Have they found her yet?"

"I don't know. I haven't heard. I'm sure they'll let us know as soon as they know something."

He squeezed her hand and she found comfort in that.

"You were bleeding badly but one of the girls had been studying for her nurse's license when she was abducted. She helped me keep the bleeding under control. We found a cell phone on one of Rayburn's goons and called Kent for help. It was touch-and-go there for a while. I wasn't sure if you were going to make it." He took a deep breath. "I almost lost you again, Rebecca."

"You didn't. I'm still here."

He touched her face and Rebecca saw true fear glistening in his eyes. He loved her. She had no doubts about that now. No matter what happened, she would never doubt that again.

His face darkened. "But I need to tell you about the money from your father."

"You don't have to explain, Collin."

"Yes, I do. I owe you the truth. I was so angry at how everything had turned out. I was angry at myself and at God and even at you because I couldn't give you what I thought you deserved. I looked at men like your dad and it seemed like having money made everything right again. I wanted that. I was so tired of struggling. So I took that money and paid the medical bills.

"It took me a long time to figure it out, but I finally learned that being a good man didn't depend on the amount of money you had in the bank but on the love you have in your heart. And I love you, Rebecca, and I'm sorry. I'm so sorry for leaving you the way I did."

She placed her hand on his lips to stop him from speaking. "It's time we put the past behind us, Collin. I'm ready to focus on the future instead."

"I'll never leave you again," he whispered to her and Rebecca took comfort in those words.

Collin was back by her side and the future looked bright again.

EPILOGUE

Rebecca was washing dishes when she spotted Collin's car pull into the driveway. She made certain Matthew was playing in the living room as she walked to the door. It had been a month since the incident at the warehouse. David had been arrested and agreed to tell what he knew about the baby-selling operation. She'd also heard from her father that David's business deals had placed his company in a very precarious situation, yet she knew her father would bounce back with some goodwill from the community.

Collin approached and drew her into a hug. "Have you heard anything?" she asked him, knowing that he'd spent the morning with Kent and the FBI.

"So far, everything David has told them has checked out. The FBI raided another operation in Texas that was apparently a hub station for the organization."

"That's good news. Have they found Missy? Is she alive?"

Collin's face spread into a grin. "She was in Texas. She's safe and will soon be reunited with Dylan and their baby. The organization apparently kept good records and the FBI was able to locate their baby with a family in Ohio."

Rebecca felt relief flow through her. That was the kind of news she'd been hoping to hear. She glanced at Matthew playing on the rug. "What about him? Did they find out anything about Matthew's mother?" It would break her heart to have to see her nephew go away, but she couldn't justify keeping a child from his biological mother, especially knowing she had never given him away voluntarily.

Collin sighed and nodded. "That's actually why I've been gone for so long. They were able to identify who Matthew's mother was. Unfortunately, she died a year ago from hemorrhaging during childbirth. They did their best to track down any family she had but couldn't find anyone. No mention of a father in the picture."

She glanced at Matthew. "So he's an orphan?"

"Well, legally, David is still his father, although I imagine the adoption will be voided since he obtained him illegally. But Matthew doesn't have to be alone." Collin reached for her hand. "You and I could give him a good home."

She sucked in a breath. Although they'd declared their love for one another and she'd been hoping they would have a second chance together, they hadn't spoken of it since she'd left the hospital. "You want us to adopt Matthew?"

He put his arms around her and pulled her tightly to him. "I'm saying we're getting a second chance. He should, too. I love you, Rebecca, and I'm never leaving you again. I want to spend my life with you and nothing would make me happier than marrying you and giving Matthew a home, along with a few brothers and sisters to boot."

God had truly restored to her what she'd lost. She may never understand why they'd had to be separated for all those years, but that no longer mattered. Only their future together mattered now. She was looking forward instead of backward. "It has always been my intention to be your wife, and that hasn't changed." There was just one problem with his plan. "But I can't marry you, Collin."

He gave her a confused look. "Why not?"

"Because, silly, we're already married… and about to celebrate our twelfth anniversary."

"Twelve years spent apart. I promise you that won't happen again. I'll never leave you again, Rebecca. I love you. I want to be with you. And this time, I want the whole world to know we're married. I don't want to keep it a secret any longer."

He pulled something from his pocket and Rebecca saw it was the chain with her ring on it. She thought she'd lost it. He pulled the ring from the chain and lifted her hand up to it, slipping it onto her finger.

"I want to be your husband and Matthew's father and father to a handful of brothers and sisters for Matthew. All you have to do is say you want the same."

"I love you, too, Collin." She leaned in to him and basked in the comfort of his arms. "Yes, I want to be your wife. I want all of it." She'd been alone for so long and now it seemed her dreams were finally coming true.

* * * * *

Dear Reader,

Thanks so much for joining me in book three of my Covert Operatives series. I hope you enjoyed Collin and Rebecca's story as much as I enjoyed writing it.

I love reunion stories and this one was no exception. These two characters fell in love at a very young age, but the pressures of real life tore them apart. This happens all too often these days, but thankfully, we serve a God of second chances. One of my favorite Bible verses is Joel 2:25, where God tells how He will restore to us what the locusts ate. I clung to this verse during a dark time in my life when it seemed all my hopes and plans for the future were ruined. I wondered if life could ever be good again. It was. My past mistakes do not define me and neither do yours because no matter how dark your situation seems right now, we have hope through Jesus Christ. He wants to heal your pains. He wants to rebuild your life.

I love hearing from my readers! You can contact me online through my website www.

virginiavaughanonline.com or on Facebook
at www.facebook.com/ginvaughanbooks.

Blessings!
Virginia

Get 4 FREE REWARDS!

We'll send you 2 FREE Books plus 2 FREE Mystery Gifts.

Love Inspired® books feature contemporary inspirational romances with Christian characters facing the challenges of life and love.

FREE
Value Over
$20